Lies in
the Wind

Judy Bruce

HOOSICK FALLS, NEW YORK
2018

First published in 2018 by the Merriam Press

First Edition

Copyright © 2018 by Judy Bruce
Cover design by Joseph Gentzler
Book design by Ray Merriam

ISBN 9781576386477
Library of Congress Control Number: 2017960328

This work was designed, produced, and published in
the United States of America by the

Merriam Press
489 South Street
Hoosick Falls NY 12090

E-mail: ray@merriam-press.com
Web site: merriam-press.com

For Danny

Other books by Judy Bruce

Death Steppe
Voices in the Wind
Alone in the Wind
Cries in the Wind
Fire in the Wind

Cast of Characters

Redmond Family

Howard (deceased)

Lucille/Lucy/Granny
> Howard's first wife, later marries Rusty Goblet

Children:
> **Gary** (deceased)
> **Gage**
> **Grant**
> **Greg**

Pearl
> Howard's second wife

Children:
> **Darold "Buster"**
> **Valerie "Val"**

Goblet Family

Russell "Rusty"

Lucille/Lucy/Granny (Redmond)

Children:
> **Gabrielle "Gabby"**
> **Abigail "Abby"**
> **Fred "Shiny"**
> **David "Dave"**
>> **Caleb,** son

Percival Family – Sidney

Kenneth "Kenny"

Helen (Goblet)

Children:
> **Celeste**

Ryan
Noah

Percival Family – Dexter
Edward, Jr. "Junior"
Valerie "Val" (Redmond)
  Mitchell "Mitch" son

Chapter I

LIFE calmed down a bit—I hadn't killed anyone for several weeks. And I didn't intend to shoot my new boyfriend, Jay. I spent a horrible day in jail falsely accused of murdering my last boyfriend, but I made bail and was later dismissed from charges. I continued to wallow in grief and guilt over the death of my unborn child; otherwise, life was good.

Still, as I rode my black stallion across a swath of buffalo grass, I sensed the roiling in my guts meant something was coming to invade my desolate corner of the world, also known as western Nebraska. I'd been shot at, divorced, knifed twice, and I'd solved murders and family mysteries; yeah, I knew about trouble. After I slowed Strider to a canter, I checked my smartphone for messages, but found none. I turned my horse around and spurred him to a full charge certain of one thing—the calamity now brewing would find me.

The next day passed normally, though my clients shocked me with their punctuality; still, my barometer of danger, my guts, percolated. Late in the afternoon, I stood chatting with Eldon Strumple, a retired minister, in the doorway of my law firm office when pounding sounded at the front entrance. Glenda, my receptionist, asked through the intercom who called.

Glenda turned toward me and said, "It's Celeste Percival. She's rather excited."

"Let her in," I said as I shook Eldon's hand.

As Eldon wandered over to chat with Glenda, who was preparing to leave for the day, Celeste burst through the door, paused, spotted me then ran toward me.

"Megan! My aunt and uncle are dead and they've arrested my dad!"

Well, that got my attention. I ushered her into my office and closed the door. Celeste was early twenties, with dark hair and a medium build. I met her during my jail stint.

"Okay, now take a deep breath and tell me what happened."

"Well, my mom called me and that's what she said."

"So your father was arrested for murder?"

"Yeah."

"Hang on," I said as I dialed my phone. Within a few minutes, one of my law partners, Rich Dewey, entered the room.

"Now, let's go through this step by step," I said. "Your dad has been arrested. Do they think he killed your uncle?"

"And my aunt. He went to their house because no one came to get Mitch and they didn't answer the phone."

"What police department was at the scene?" asked Rich.

"Ah, the county sheriff. But this makes no sense. My folks and my aunt and uncle always got along. Now they're dead. My God."

When she began to blurt and sob, I summoned Glenda, who brought a root beer and a cream cheese pastry.

After Celeste took a few swigs of the root beer, she said, "No sense, no damn sense. Those Redmonds always hated the Goblets and my mom is a Goblet and my aunt Val is a Redmond and Shiny Goblet would kill anyone for a buck."

Rich looked at me in utter confusion then turned to Celeste and said, "I'll go the sheriff's office to see your dad. I'll be in touch."

Rich closed the door behind him.

"Who's Shiny Goblet?" I asked.

"Fred Goblet."

"Oh, right, he operates an insurance agency in Kimball. He seems respectable enough."

"Oh, he's a snake, a'right. A slimy cheat. Got divorced because he was foolin' around on his wife. That was years ago." She heaved a great sigh. "My aunt and uncle…just can't believe it…finally getting' that room built on…and now they're dead."

"Celeste, I want you to go home. Mitch is there, isn't he?"

"Yeah. Van brings him about quarter till four."

"Then go home…help take care of him. I will go to the scene. You'll hear from me or Rich, or maybe Gus, my other partner."

"But I want to go with you," she said.

"They'll never let family get close. I don't even know if I can get in even as the family attorney. Listen, your family needs to keep Mitch, at least for now. I'll try to collect clothes and things and bring them over."

Celeste nodded as she rose and walked stiff-legged to the door. It occurred to me that I hadn't smelled smoke on her, which pleased me.

I rang Melanie Sundstrom, my Nordic-blonde paralegal, who quickly appeared at the door. I gave a quick sketch of the situation then told her to follow Celeste home.

"Wait, take this." I walked over and gave my National Geographic floor globe a spin. "Mitch loves this…the colors and the texture of the mountains. I can get a new one."

"I saw Junior and Valerie at Custer's just last week," she said.

"I know…it's horrible. Oh, let Gus in on things when his meeting ends. Thanks."

On the way to the Percival house on this chilly November day, I thought about Edward "Junior" Percival and Valerie Percival. Last week, they'd brought in Mitch, their only child, a profoundly autistic, mentally retarded, nonverbal youngster of fifteen. That poor boy—he struggled greatly with change, so the permanent disappearance of his parents would hit him hard. As I neared the Percival house, my hands began to sweat. I'd never visited a murder scene—well, except for the ones I'd participated in. Three Cheyenne County Sheriff Department cruisers were parked in the street blocking traffic. So I parked a block away. Onlookers gathered in the yards. An ambulance was parked backwards in the single-lane driveway behind a silver pickup truck I assumed to be Junior's. The Dexter police car was parked directly in the front of the house—the presence of our chief of police heartened me.

Chief Tate McNeill met me as I approached the sidewalk of the narrow, light beige, single-story house.

"Megan, I don't know if they'll let you in," he said.

"Well, let me try."

The moment I approached the front porch, the county sheriff and one of his deputies crowded me to a stop.

"What do you think you're doing?" said Sheriff Stan Smythe.

"Do you know Mitch?" I asked.

"I know about him," said the burly cop.

"Then you know he's epileptic."

"Ah, right."

"Now that boy is going to suffer greatly over a loss he'll never understand. I don't think he needs seizures on top of the deaths of his parents, do you?"

The sheriff scratched his late-day whiskers.

"I'm here to collect meds and clothing for Mitch. I'm also his attorney and the attorney for the Percival estate. Now, I'm asking that you allow me to enter this house. Chief McNeill can supervise me." I handed him my card.

"You will not disturb or take photos of the crime scenes," said the sheriff.

"I have no legal interest in the criminal aspects of the case. I do plan to bag up several of Mitch's toys and DVDs, with your permission and inspection, of course."

"All right, make it quick," said Sheriff Smythe.

LIES IN THE WIND

As soon as I stepped into the front room, I heard him—a gasp of surprise then a grunt. And I felt it—evil. Cold and terrible. Then I saw him—flat on his back, blood had run down from the bullet hole under Junior's chin onto his neck, staining his sweatshirt collar dark. Blood had pooled beside him on the wood floorboards and the edge had been smudged. Blood was splattered on the taupe wall behind him. A rifle lay on the floor next to him, but not in his hand. My God.

I knew this man. He was no more. Why?

Chief Tate gently tugged my arm and I walked with him. But leaving the room gave me no relief—the house was thick with menace and pain; fear hung in the air as we entered the kitchen. The second death happened here—I knew it before I saw her.

A scream jolted me to a stop. She had screamed in terror, gasped, and then gurgled. I stepped forward and peered around the kitchen table. Val was slumped against the door to their bedroom, a dark hole in her forehead. She wasn't bloody, but a dark smudge was visible on the left side of her neck. Her head was propped up by the frame of the door, her arms hung down at her side, and her left leg was straight out in front of her as the other was bent so that her foot rested against the inside of her left knee. Along the inside of the pant leg was a dark spot and the sole of her gray slipper showed a dark smudge. Like Junior, she wore jeans, but with a royal blue fleece pullover, probably the clothes they changed into after work. My phone buzzed inside my purse, but I ignored it.

"The evil just hangs in the air," I said.

"Um, right," said Chief Tate. "The Sheriff says Junior must have shot her, shoved her against the door…she's got bruises on both sides of her neck. Then he went into the front room and shot himself."

"But that can't be. I know these people…I mean, not close…but it doesn't seem right."

My whole body went to lead. Chief Tate pulled me to a cupboard in the kitchen.

"Ah, right. Meds." I started opening the cupboard doors.

"Here," Tate said as he looked into a cupboard beside the sink.

On the inside of a door was a list of medications, their dosages, and the schedule of times for administration. Prozac, Seroquel, Risperdal, Depakote, multivitamin, Miralax, melatonin—no wonder they needed a list. I found a box of plastic bags. I started loading the stash of bottles into the sack. Tate gently pulled down the list from the door and added it to the bags. I took it to the front door where I set it down for the deputies to investigate. The sheriff walked over to me.

"Judge Shelton is a family friend. I'm going to tell him of your good judgment in allowing Chief and me to get these items for Mitch…or would that get you in trouble?"

He nodded to me. "That would be fine, Miz Docket."

When I walked back to the kitchen, Tate was grinning at me.

"Quite the diplomat," he whispered.

This time I didn't look at Val, I took another plastic bag and handed one to Tate. We walked into the adjoining TV room and bagged books, several colorful balls, and DVDs, especially the Disney and Pixar ones. In Mitch's bedroom at the front of the house, we bagged his winter clothes, shoes, and boots. Then I paused to think about Mitch; change upset him, so how could I lessen that? I convinced Tate to bag up Mitch's pillows while I folded his comforter. Kenny and Helen, his uncle and aunt, would become his new parents. What would help them? I added Mitch's night light which had a cover shaped like a blue football and a stuffed panda that sat on his dresser. Tate went over and picked up the stuffed tiger and lion that sat in his otherwise sparsely decorated room; lots of toys or books would probably distract the quirky kid as he tried to settle down for sleep.

As we piled the bags by the front door, my phone buzzed. One of the deputies looked over at me, but I ignored the call. He went back to inspecting the bags.

"We should do a once-through in case we missed something that could help Helen with Mitch," I said as much for the sheriff as for Tate. "She will become his new mother."

"What about photos?" asked Tate.

"No, I don't think so. It's cruel, but he needs to forget them."

The sheriff looked at me for a moment then turned away as his face reddened. I sympathized with his plight, for I was ready to run screaming from the house of grunts and screams and evil; I took a deep breath to steady myself. I'd gained the trust of the county police—now it was time for a bit of stealth. I went back to the kitchen and over to the roll-top desk in the corner, trying my best to ignore Val's screams. As the deputies were inspecting the bags at the front door, I began to look through the various piles of envelopes and cubby holes, though was careful not to touch their laptop. Tate watched as I rolled up then shoved papers into my oversized purse.

"I'm playing attorney now," I whispered to Tate.

"You shouldn't be doing this," he whispered back. "But Rachel says to trust you."

I rifled through the drawers as Tate kept watch on the deputies. Rachel was a friend of mine, a State Patrol officer, and his ex-wife. I finished, closed the desk, and went into the TV room and through a door to the bathroom and laundry room. As expected in a bungalow, a house without halls, another door let out into the master bedroom. At their dresser, I started moving my hands through their unmentionables. Tate gave me a look.

"I haven't found the will or codicil. I need the originals. I'm the executor and neither Kenny nor Helen know it. They'll assume they are."

My hand stopped then drew out a Docket Law envelope. I shoved it into my purse and closed the drawer just as I heard the approaching heavy footsteps of the sheriff. I didn't look at him but backed up as I looked around the room.

I gave him a glance, then said, "It seems like Mitch should have something of theirs...but maybe not. I just don't know. Sheriff, any ideas?"

Once again, I put him on his heels—he was supposed to be acting the smart cop, but he'd never probably supervised a murder scene and the father in him kept surfacing. He was a good man, but not smart enough to keep me in check.

In the silence, I said, "I gotta get out of here."

I strode past the men and back through the cramped bathroom past the stacked washer and dryer combo that included a load of clothes that would never get folded. I was working and thinking, yet this event was a kick that made my guts ache. I walked past the TV room into the under-construction north addition. My friends Lew and Hank Eldritch were the carpenters for the interior of the room built by Troff Construction. The company finished building, roofing, and painting the exterior just before the early winter hit. Now the room smelled of drywall dust and insulation. The framing was complete, and half of the drywall was in place along the walls. Some sections of the drywall had not been added where electrical sockets existed. A four by four foot plywood box was set into the drywall on the west side of the room. Canvas drop clothes were rolled up next to stacks of wood planks and drywall piled in the center of the plywood flooring.

When Tate and the sheriff approached, I said, "Lord, it's nice to get away from them. I wonder what they planned for the floor."

When we all looked down at the floor in unison, I felt like we were the Three Stooges in the house of murder, a movie nobody would ever have filmed. The room was cold—I wondered why the single glass-paned door would have been left open, for it would let cold air from the partially-insulated room into the rest of the house.

"Did one of your deputies open this door?" I asked.

The sheriff shrugged. "It was open when I got here."

Something seemed wrong here, not the open door, something else. What was the cause of my churning guts? Danger? I walked over to the north windows to make it look like I was viewing the backyard, but I needed to do it quickly. The sheriff wanted me to go.

Danger. That was it. But it didn't make sense. I did take a few moments to look over the yard. A massive English oak was only ten feet from the house. I was no tree expert, but the house seemed too close to such a tree, one of the oldest in town. A huge branch even extended past the western corner of the house; the roots probably extended under this portion of the house, but maybe that wasn't a problem as the basement wouldn't extend past the original foundation. But why did I feel danger?

Even in November, the English oak still had half its green leaves when many other trees had lost all of theirs. In any other year, Junior would be raking leaves into early January. Val once told me that Mitch like picking up the acorns that fell from the tree during the fall. But for now, the few inches of snow were disturbed by only a few leaves and small branches the wind dislodged. Although I didn't have any reason, except for my snooping instinct, I opened the inside back door then pushed open the storm door and looked out onto the cement porch and sidewalk. A single set of footprints ran along the sidewalk to the left, though they looked to end at the corner of the house. A wooden, six-foot, fold-out ladder was propped against the house. It looked as though someone recently used it to inspect the exterior of the house. Junior probably needed to keep the gutter clear of acorns, branches, and leaves as the upper portion of the oak extended over the single-story house.

"What?" asked the sheriff, with a bit of irritation in his voice.

"Oh, ah, it just doesn't seem like a good idea to build a house under a huge, old tree in Tornado Alley," I said as I closed and locked both doors. "Well, I'm ready to get out of here. I need to deliver all that stuff to the Percival's."

"Sheriff!" yelled a deputy.

Sheriff Smythe turned and ran out of the room. Tate and I followed.

Back in the front room, a deputy stood next to Junior's body.

"I spotted that pocket knife on the floor there, behind his back. He carved into the wood floor before he died."

"What does it say?" asked the sheriff.

"It says, 'Sorry.'"

"All right, come out from there."

The deputy walked along the sofa away from the body and purposefully stood in front of me. The sheriff turned to look at me, either irritated that I'd heard about that bit of information or embarrassed that they'd been so slow to discover it, or maybe both.

"Not a word," he said.

"Sheriff, you forget—I'm an attorney, not a reporter. My job is to keep secrets, not spread them." I turned to Tate and said, "Chief, will you help me haul these bags out to my SUV?"

As I pulled away from the house of death in my Acura SUV, the Barracuda, I turned off the heat. I welcomed the cold air that distracted me from the horror of that scene. Now I needed to focus on my next dreadful task.

Chapter 2

WHEN I arrived at the Percival home, a pale gray two-story, I backed the SUV into their driveway for easy unloading of the bags. Rich Dewey was waiting for me in the driveway.

"Kenny was never actually arrested," said Rich. "He was just so upset that one of the deputies took him to the station for a cup of coffee. I've known Kenny for several years so when I say he was upset, I mean he became a major a-hole."

"I can't say I blame him," I said. "That scene is a nightmare. The sheriff thinks Junior shot Val then shot himself. 'Sorry' was etched into the wood floor by Junior's body. But I just...I don't know what to think."

Celeste stood with Helen and Kenny, on their front porch, shivering in the cold wind.

"The back of my car is full of stuff for Mitch," I said as I handed Helen the bag of Mitch's meds.

"Three reporters have already called to pester us," said Kenny as I followed him inside.

Like his brother, Kenny was of medium build, mid-forties, with light brown hair thinning on top and a beard they both kept full, but trimmed. Junior, the elder, was a nice guy, whereas Kenny was known as a jerk. I gave Celeste's arm a squeeze and she nodded to me.

"Noah and Ryan came home early from football practice to be with Mitch," said Helen.

The Sidney Percivals lived in a nicer house than Junior and Val. Kenny was a foreman at the root beer brewery. I was soon seated on their living room sofa with a cup of coffee. Helen was short and chunky, a contrast to Val, who was nearly five foot ten. I thought of Val, still propped up against the door. Fear—it had been heavy in that room. I wondered if the deputies figured out they needed to take photographs and measurements of the scenes and bodies. When Rich gave me a nudge, I became aware I'd missed Kenny's question.

"I'm sorry," I said. "I guess I'm still in shock."

"Those cops wouldn't let me past the front room. Dammit! There's no way Junior could have killed Val. No way. I never saw Val—"

I realized that was a question. "She was in the kitchen." I looked into their faces and knew they expected more. "Listen, I'm not a detective. Yes, the sheriff thinks Junior shot Val then shot himself. But I promise you this—I will be talking with the State Patrol about this. Not that the sheriff has done anything wrong, but something like this needs to investigated to the hundredth degree. Everything needs to be crystal clear. Also, Dexter Chief Tate McNeill is on the scene. He's knows his stuff."

Heads nodded.

"How's Mitch?" I asked.

"He knows something is out of whack. He knows he should be home. But Ryan thought Star Wars would amuse him and it has." Helen dabbed her eyes. "That poor boy."

"I brought everything I could of his. I left the car unlocked."

Kenny walked into family room down the hall to the sound of blasters and Han Solo. Ryan and Noah, muscular athletes, glanced at me then followed their father out the front door.

Celeste rose. "Megan, would you like to see him?"

"Yes, but he may not need another face to deal with."

So I followed Celeste and peeked around the corner at Mitch, who glanced at Celeste then back at the screen. Mitch was trim and five ten or so with dark hair like his mother. The globe from my office was next to him. Every now and then he reached over and gave it a spin, often without looking at it. I backed up and strode down the hall trying to tamp down the ball of emotion lodged in my esophagus. I needed to be strong and helpful for these people. I could cry for Mitch later.

"Mitch will sleep with Noah tonight," said Helen, whose face was reddened with emotion. "He has a double bed."

Piles of bags began to accumulate in the front room.

"I brought Mitch's pillows and comforter. I thought he might like that. Um, I'm gonna go. I'll keep in touch. Tell Celeste to eat chocolate."

Helen smiled. "She told me you ate chocolate in the jail together."

I grabbed her hand. "This is going to be tough in so many ways. Take care of yourself."

I appreciated the sting of the cold air as I walked out to the Barracuda.

Elated to be home, I wished I didn't have a crowd waiting for me. Uncle Bill and my mom, Beth, who were now married and living a block down the street, stood in the kitchen with Patty White Horse, my Lakota housekeeper and former nanny. For the first time, I realized that it was after seven. They had waited supper on me. I washed my hands then plopped down at the kitchen table.

"I'm sorry I didn't call," I said. "I was at the scene then I brought Mitch's things to the Percival house in Sidney."

Mom took my purse off my shoulder. "No problem. We kept the steaks warm."

Blood seeping into the floor boards. Stench like rotting meat. Bruises. An orphan. At least I didn't see their open eyes up close.

Uncle Bill set a snifter of brandy in front of me. "You need this."

I took a swig and felt the warmth spread down my throat. Another swallow brought the warmth into my arms. James. I put the glass down. This had been the favorite libation of my beloved neighbor and friend. He died last month—as I watched. Patty set in front of me a small plate with three chocolate truffles. I couldn't help but smile. Bill pushed the snifter back toward me. I took another sip, ate a truffle, and closed my eyes, feeling blessed and tended to. Lord above, please help the Percival family.

Soon supper was set before us and a forced attempt at small talk ensued to keep my mind off dreadful thoughts and on my dinner. Patty even tried to bribe me, promising me more chocolate truffles if I finished my broccoli. That worked. Then Bill tried to bait me with brandy if I finished my steak. That didn't work.

After supper, we settled into the family room. I quickly checked the phone messages I'd received and ignored earlier. One was from Mom and the other was a text from Jay saying he'd be working late. Again, small talk was attempted, but it was so strained I stopped eating truffles long enough to say what I needed to.

"I saw them at the scene. It was horrible." I then provided a very brief description.

Silence followed.

In time, Bill blurted, "That just can't be! No way does Junior Percival kill anybody, especially Val. Theirs was a good marriage. Mitch just pulled them closer together."

"Megan, what did you feel when you were there?" asked Patty, who was always the one who wanted to tap into my oddness.

"Evil. Surprise. Fear."

I flushed hot and woozy. Bill set a generous portion of brandy in front of me. James would have said I needed a restorative and he was right.

"Seems like I should have seen more. But the shock of it made my brain sloggy. It was my first murder scene."

I looked up—everyone had frozen.

I smiled. "I mean those other times there wasn't any mystery...I knew what happened. But this one..." I shook my head.

"Megan, are you thinking the sheriff is wrong that it's a murder and suicide?" asked Mom.

Did I think it was wrong? Something was itching at me. Then I remembered the danger I'd sensed. Why would I feel danger at a scene where the killing was already done?

"I-I'm not sure. Maybe."

Nobody could draw anything more out of me after that, so the group broke up. Patty offered to stay over, but I thanked her and declined.

I lay in bed staring at the gas fireplace. It gave me comfort; I often turned it on before bedtime to ease my way to sleep when I was haunted; but I also knew not to turn away from it, for the shadows it cast on the other side of the room could bring on a trembling fit. Yes, I could recall the nightmares and the day mares of post-traumatic stress. Killing two cops horrified me, even if it was done impulsively and deservedly—I'd provoked DEA Agent RT Martin to reach for his gun then I shot him bloody dead; I'd then wrapped my hand around the gun in RT's death grip hand and pushed down on his finger to fire into Police Chief Dobbs. They killed Davey, the autistic young man who'd worked at Custer's diner. I was fond of Davey; I never forgave myself for not anticipating his murder when he innocently repeated information he heard regarding RT's drug operation.

Now here was Mitch, another autistic boy, but fifteen years of age with the intelligence, maturity, and judgment of a toddler. His neurologic dysfunction made him ninety times more complicated than any normal child. Now his world was shattered.

It felt wrong, I finally admitted it. Murder then suicide—why was it wrong when it looked that way? What made me think otherwise? Oh, how tired I was in mind and body. Sleep would do me so much good, but I couldn't stop myself from visualizing each body, each inch of that horrific scene. Why didn't I see and understand more when I was there?

I pulled the extra pillow over my head, which calmed me, to my surprise. I could still peek through the slit in the pillows at the fireplace as the gas flames flicked upward, over and over, and over....

Deep in the night, I popped to a sitting position, heart pounding, pillow flying off the far side of the bed.

The smear!

It was so obvious. Why was I so stupid? I rolled over to the edge of the far side of the bed and grabbed the phone. Jay responded with a groggy greeting.

"Jay, it's the smear! That's what's wrong. Maybe I was thinking so much about Mitch and sneaking around that I didn't think. Yes, it was stupid of me."

"Megan, stop. Now tell me what you're talking about. And do you know it's four in the morning?"

"It's not a murder-suicide."

"You mean the Percivals. Okay, um, that's for the county sheriff...but what are you saying?"

"It was a double murder. The Sheriff concluded that Junior killed his wife then himself. But she had a dark smear on the bottom of her slipper that looked like blood. She didn't bleed."

"So the blood she stepped in must have been his," he said.

"Chief Tate said she had bruise marks around her throat because he grabbed her. I'm so, so stupid. But there's someone out there who murdered two people. Listen, the county is going to screw this up."

"Still, it's their jurisdiction."

"But a source of mine named a suspect from Kimball County, which is outside their jurisdiction. The State Patrol has to take over this case. Jay, the Sheriff saw what he was meant to see. But it's bloody wrong."

"Are you willing to name your source?"

"If I need to."

"Man alive. Um, okay. It's too early to contact the sheriff. And I won't be going back to sleep."

"Me neither."

"You know, you're really sexy when you're smart."

"I was stupid till now."

"Should I come over?" he asked.

"Two people got murdered today, er, yesterday and you want to make love?"

"No."

"Me neither." In truth, figuring out that two murders had been committed gave me the heebie-jeebies; still, I wanted the comfort of a warm-bodied man who carried a gun.

"I'll brush and be over."

Jay was in my bed with me in record time. No doubt he'd driven faster than a lieutenant in the State Patrol should have. But he was warm and buff and hairy-chested. I ran my fingers over the nighttime whiskers of his strong jaw then kissed his dimpled chin.

"Hmmm, flannel jammies," he said.

"Well, it's cold in here alone. Maybe you ought to do something about them."

He did, button by button, kiss by kiss. I shouldn't have been able to focus on him, on our love-making, but I did with relish.

I was crazy about this man. He grasped my quirks and my qualities and my penchant for trouble—and accepted me. I'd seen him at work—issuing orders, giving information, praising, warning, inspiring his officers. I knew several troopers so I'd heard even the veteran cops respected him though he was only thirty-five. Yet this hard-charging boss-man transformed into a laid-back, easily amused man who enjoyed lounging on my sofa with me, chatting with my Harney Street gang. He was secure in his own skin—it didn't bother him that I was a boss, too, and I had killed more men than he had, well, the last one was actually a woman. I didn't intimidate him, not even with my weird sensory perception. I had never been more comfortable with a man.

As I lay under his hot flesh, soaking in the reverberations of our excitement, I said with a smirk, "You know, I wasn't a virgin our first time."

"I hope not," he said. "You'd have made a lousy wife."

"You erase them."

He lifted his head to stare at me, his mouth open, breathing quick shallow breaths. He swallowed me with a wet kiss then dropped his head into my neck. He stayed that way for nine thousand lovely hours then slid his arms under my back and rolled over, bringing me with him. He kept his face in my neck, though I wanted to see it. I waited; finally, he lifted his head, pierced me with his blue eyes, kissed me, and then scooped me off the bed and took me to the shower. I guess I'd hit the mark.

Yet, it hit us both the moment we left the bedroom for breakfast. The day would be horrible, we both sensed it. After toast and scrambled eggs, he left for work, while I went back upstairs to change out of my robe and fleece slippers into my work pantsuit. I knew I'd be going back to the scene, Jay promised he would summon me. So I took a few minutes to pray for comfort, strength, and clarity before I headed to the Barracuda.

LIES IN THE WIND

Chapter 3

AFTER I finished discussing a motor vehicle accident with a new client from Banner County, Jay called.

"It's ours," he said. "The sheriff admitted the brown substance on Valerie's slipper was probably blood and a problem with his conclusion of a murder-suicide. I don't think he was all that bothered by losing the case because he's short two officers...out with sinus infections...and he has to deal with last night's nasty three-car accident north of Potter on one of our many open intersections."

"Okay, good, so who's going to be at the house?"

"Well, Merritt and McNeill for sure. I'm getting ready to leave. I viewed the bodies in the morgue. We're waiting on toxicology tests."

"I'll meet you there," I said.

When I arrived at the Percival house, an unfamiliar State Patrol cop stood outside the door, so I waited in my SUV for Jay. Soon, Sergeant Warren Merritt, Officer Rachel McNeill, and Chief Tate McNeill arrived. I met them on the driveway. When Jay joined us, he asked why we hadn't gone inside.

"I can tell you what I saw and felt, but I can't do it in front of a stranger," I said. "Send him to interview the neighbors or something."

"Aren't you making a big deal out of this?" asked Jay. "I've got another man inside. It was hard getting this many officers assigned to this case."

I looked him in the eye then turned and walked back to my SUV, angrier with each step. I'd already figured out what the county sheriff and four deputies couldn't. The hell with you, buddy. Figure it out yourself. I was ready to risk letting familiar cops think I was nuts, I didn't plan on exposing myself to others. Just as I opened the door, Jay called after me. I got inside anyway and started the engine. Merritt blocked my exit, apologized, and convinced me to come back. We'd been through several of my "incidents" together and he'd acted like a big brother to me when I was in jail.

When I rejoined the group in the driveway, I said, "I can't work with strangers and I can't work with pricks." Then I turned and walked toward the house.

Jay caught up with me. "Megan, c'mon."

"Why is it that you get stupid when you put on the uniform? You did it last month with Waters. Now go get rid of those other cops. I'll talk to Rachel and Merritt."

I stopped on the sidewalk. It was bloody cold, but I wasn't going inside until I was ready. Jay went into the house and within a few minutes both cops passed me on the sidewalk. I paused on the front step.

"The sheriff stopped me here, but I convinced him that Mitch, being autistic and epileptic, needed his meds. He let me in. He's a father, I can tell." I opened the door and stepped into the room with Jay in front of me and Merritt, Rachel, and Tate behind me. "Before I even saw Junior, I felt the tremendous evil that hung in the air. Then I heard him, Junior that is, his gasp of surprise then a grunt then nothing. Of course, what I say is all in confidence."

I took a breath and looked over to the chalked outline of his body, the pool of blood on the wood floor, "Sorry" etched into the wood.

"The deputies nearly missed that carving. I never saw the pocket knife...it must have been under the body. So if this is a murder then the killer etched that into the wood as a suicide note. And isn't this a lot of blood for a shot to the head?"

"Junior may have got his hand on the rifle just enough to deflect it a bit," said Merritt. "The shot went though the neck hitting the carotid artery, but missing the brain. Otherwise, there wasn't much of a struggle."

"Does it still feel like evil in here?" asked Rachel.

"Yeah, not as strong, but I still hear his gasp and his grunt and sense of surprise."

"Maybe Junior knew the killer and didn't know to be afraid," said Rachel. "Even though the perp would have been holding a gun."

"Maybe he asked Junior a question about it," said Merritt. "He wasn't surprised till the barrel of the rifle is rammed under his throat. Even then, he must have fired quickly to avoid a fight."

Rachel took a notebook out of her coat and started scribbling notes. I walked toward the kitchen, past Jay, without looking at him. He was a hindrance—I wished he wasn't here.

"The sense of evil continues into this room. But then fear explodes. And Val—" I gasped and leaned against the threshold of the door. Jay stepped to my side, but I waved him back.

"Screams. Junior was killed first then the murderer came for her. She must have been in the room with Junior when he was shot for her to step in his blood. She ran into the kitchen and started to scream."

"We don't have any reports of gunfire or anything else from the neighbors," said Merritt.

I looked back at the TV in the front room.

"Yeah, you hear gunfire on TV a lot," said Merritt. "And the windows would be closed."

"And you have elderly neighbors on both sides of this house." I turned back to the kitchen and the screams. "One of them was at my office."

Jay was staring at the chalk outline of the body. "This isn't very good."

"Well, she was slumped," I said. "See, there's the bullet hole in the door above her."

I sat down on the floor and leaned back against the doors under the sink. I bent my right leg in and put my head to the side.

"That's exactly how she was," said Tate.

"So the killer grabs her neck and pushes her against the door," said Jay.

"Oh, wait." I bent my left foot toward the floor. "Val was duck-footed, so her foot was almost on the floor. I can't even bend my foot that far without changing my posture."

Rachel said, "And her legs stretch out several inches farther than yours."

"Yeah, she was tall, just about Junior's height…taller in heels." I stood up. "Then Chief Tate and I start collecting Mitch's meds from that cabinet."

To demonstrate, Tate opened the cupboard.

"Then we get toys and DVDs from this next room. By then, the cops stop worrying about me, so I grab stuff from her piles of papers at the desk here and go into their bedroom and find the will I drafted awhile back. It was supposed to be in a safety deposit box, but it was in his sock drawer."

"You aren't supposed to take things from a crime scene," said Jay.

"Of course not," I said with a shrug. "But I'm their attorney and the executor of the estate, but that's a secret. Kenny, the brother, won't be happy when he learns that. And as slow as the cops were moving, I didn't know when I'd ever get access to their papers. Don't worry, you'll get them back. Those deputies looked traumatized. Did they remember to take photos?"

"I had to remind them," said Tate. "And no one wore booties. It was shoddy supervision of the scene."

I nodded then walked through the TV room and into the north addition. "This door was open when I was here, though that's pretty stupid since it's cold and this room is only partially insulated."

Everybody followed me into the room.

"Now the sounds I heard from Val and Kenny make sense with the likely events of the murders. But something still baffles me." I took a breath. "When I walked in here, more than evil, I sensed danger."

"Danger?" asked Jay.

"Yeah, danger. I don't get that. And how does the killer get in and out? The snow was undisturbed around the house."

I walked over to the north windows. I looked out over the snow-covered lawn. But now the yard had a quantity of leaves and branches down. I dashed over to the door, but paused before I touched the handle.

"Tate! Look at all the leaves down, but they're only on that far side."

"You're right," he said. "I don't get that."

"I need to see the sidewalk outside, but this door shouldn't be opened."

"You mean it needs to be dusted for fingerprints," said Rachel.

"Yeah." I grabbed Rachel's notebook from her hand and set it against the glass of the window and pressed my head against it. "There's more footprints back here than there were yesterday. Maybe the deputies did that. But yesterday, a single set of footprints led from this door to the edge of the house or the other way around. Junior hadn't bothered to shovel back here. Now it looks like two sets of prints. Yesterday, I opened the door to look. There was also a wood, six-foot ladder up against the house." I moved back to the door. "This back door was unlocked yesterday. I locked it after I looked outside. Strange, but I know I locked the storm door, too. Now it's unlocked. The deputies must have been here."

Jay took Merritt aside and talked to him. Merritt strode out of the room.

"Well, that's all I know," I said backing away from the windows. "Odd pattern of leaves coming down with those branches, but just on one side. Is this how the killer came and went? He'd have to be Spiderman. Oh, yeah, there's a laptop in the roll-top desk. Okay, I'm going back to work."

I said my goodbyes and left. Jay got a call, which prevented him from running after me. I needed to get out of the house of murder as fast as I could. I went back to work then home for lunch. I wasn't ready for an inquisition at Custer's.

After work, I spent time in my study at home, sorting through the bills, personal papers, and other information I swiped from the Percival house. Junior and Val weren't wage earners of significance, but they lived within their means and paid their bills on time. I had swiped a few personal letters that I set aside to be read only if necessary. Of all the papers I nabbed from the Percival house, one stood out—a single page of correspondence regarding a life insurance policy in Val's name. The page listed a policy number, but not the death benefit amount or the beneficiaries. The page stated it was the first of two pages. Where was the second page? Fortunately, the insurance company was State Farm.

Our firm had handled motor vehicle accident claims for State Farm for over two decades. The insurance company needed to determine if the insured meant to commit suicide—life insurance policies typically become invalid if the insured party committed suicide within the first two years of the policy issuance. If the Percival policy had been issued within the last two years, an investigation would need to be conducted. Even if the policy was a long-standing one, I'd probably be able to find out the death benefit amount and the beneficiaries, even if it was off the record. I'd give the superintendant in North Platte a call tomorrow morning. I photocopied all the papers, put the copies in an envelope and the originals in another.

As I was organizing the papers, Jay called and asked if he could come over. In fact, he was parked in my driveway. I locked the Percival papers in my desk, set a will on my desk and folded back the first page, and then I went to the front door to let him in. Patty was in the family room watching a Western. She loved them, though mocking them was her second favorite pastime.

I led Jay into the study, assuming he wanted to talk about our clash earlier in the day.

"You thought I was a stupid cop today," he said. "But you defied me in front of my officers."

"I'm not your employee."

"You called me a 'prick.'"

"I agree that was harsh, but this is touchy stuff…not just the murders…but with me. I thought you were incredibly insensitive. You don't get it."

"What don't I get?"

"Look, I know I am weird, but I think I have the right to choose the people who witness my…oddness. Most people would think I'm nuts. Maybe I am. But even Merritt and Rachel and particularly Tate heard more of my weirdness than they ever had. I usually just say I know something and then never answer why. But this was murder, so I decided to put myself out there. Those other two cops would have gone back to the station blabbing about what a nut case I am."

"It's not weirdness. It's insight."

"It doesn't matter what you call it…it's personal. Merritt probably calls it useful insanity."

"Well, I'm sorry I was clumsy about it."

I nodded then put the will back in a drawer. I handed Jay the envelope with original papers I took from the Percival house.

"Look, I'm all played out tonight," I said.

"I understand. But one thing, all of this has to be kept in confidence."

I stared at him. No kidding.

"But you know that."

I held my tongue.

"Are you still mad at me?"

"It takes time for people to get to know one another," I said with all the tact I could muster. "Goodnight."

He stood while I stayed seated at my desk. He waited, but I wasn't planning to budge—my turf, my say. His waiting began to annoy me. He thought a hug and a kiss would bend me.

"I think we should end our discussions on the murders. I'll keep in touch with Rachel or Merritt. This isn't working for us." I took the will out of the desk and turned to the second page.

He backed up slowly then left.

I felt lousy. Maybe when he got to know me better, he wouldn't be such a clumsy oaf. If he stayed this way, we were in trouble. Maybe he thought sex would fix a problem. Or maybe he thought we should just forget about things, have sex, and then later deal with an issue. I could gloss over little things, but I couldn't just push a double murder out of my mind like it didn't happen. Then again, if I didn't tell Jay thoughts like these, how could he understand me better?

Still, it disturbed me that I was the one who proved the murder-suicide wrong. Would the killer find out about that? Shit. People would question why the State Patrol took over the investigation from the county sheriff. I downed a handful of Rolaids.

I opened a side drawer, lifted the cover of a box, and then set my Glock on the corner of the desk.

Chapter 4

B Y late morning, I received a response from State Farm—an email from Superintendant Albert Carlsson requesting an investigation of the circumstances surrounding the death of Valerie A. Percival. Attachments included a copy of the policy issued seven months ago and a letter from Al advising of my assignment as a representative of State Farm Life Insurance Company regarding the life insurance benefits claim. He also stated that if Edward Percival, Jr. had an insurance policy, it wasn't with State Farm. Val's policy listed the primary beneficiary as Edward R. Percival, Jr. husband. Mitchell K. Percival, child, and Darold H. Redmond, brother, were indicated as equal secondary beneficiaries. I didn't even know Val had a brother, for she never mentioned him and she hadn't included him in her will. Now I was officially involved in the investigation. But where was Darold?

I started to call Helen, but hesitated. Did I really want to reveal the existence of the life insurance money when neither she nor Kenny benefitted directly? Eventually, they would legally become Mitch's guardians and conservators, who maintained custody of him and supervised his finances. However, that was down the road after filings with the county court and their appearances at hearings. Still, I needed to proceed with probate. Mitch would need funds for his care; also, as executor, I controlled their assets so I needed to get outstanding debts paid, the autos and the house sold, and generally account for the finances of the estate. I needed to meet with Kenny and Helen and advise them I was the executor, not them, as the original wills stated. However, when I called Helen to schedule a meeting, she was less than cordial.

"Listen, Miss Docket, we thank you for bringing Mitch his things, but this is our business now."

"You think so? Well, you know where to find me. My office hours are eight to five. Goodbye."

Two murders. Darold Redmond was Val's brother, so she must be a Redmond. The feud between the Redmonds and the Goblets was infamous in our corner of the world. Celeste had suggested Fred Goblet was the murderer even before she knew any of the facts of the deaths. Though it wasn't a large life insurance benefit, it would be a lot of money for most people around here.

Twenty-five grand, fifty total—would someone commit murder for either sum?

I called Jay and invited him over for supper; he declined because of a late meeting, but promised to come afterward.

"Oh, and have you interviewed Hank and Lew?" I asked.

"Not yet, but we will today," he said.

"May I make a suggestion?"

"Sure."

"Send Rachel. Lew's scared of cops. Maybe he won't be scared of her. Though he can be scared of women...especially my mom...at least till she got married."

"They both should be scared of cops—they've both done time. Nothing terrible, just jail time for fighting...twice for Hank."

"I wondered about Hank and I knew Lew spent time in jail for fighting at the Cowpoke. He was protecting his drunken brother."

"Salt, the one you later killed."

"In self-defense and thanks for reminding me."

"Sorry, I'm just trying to be open and honest," he said.

"Try using a filter. You come off more clumsy than sincere."

"I'm sorry."

He was quiet for a few moments, but I waited.

"It's just that you come off so tough, deadly even, but then you're so sensitive about things."

"Don't think of it as tough...it tortures me greatly. Think of those "incidents" like I just responded in a satisfactory way to unfortunate circumstances."

"Okay, got it."

I wondered, did he?

At eleven-thirty the next day, Mom and I met Patty at the Docket booth at Custer's. My mom had accepted a job at my office as support staff after I added a third attorney to the firm. However, she spent most mornings helping people get signed up with the new health care law. She had taken over Melanie's desk as I'd cut Brian's office space in half, which allowed me to give Melanie an office. Brian was the accountant who rented office space from Docket Law. Since our divorce, he spent more time at his Sidney office, a twenty-minute drive away.

The diner possessed a strange buzz of conversation, lower and more solemn, now a day and half after the deaths of the Percivals. Carol took our order and Beulah, my elderly friend, shuffled our way.

"We all heard you were at the scene," said a voice nearby.

I glared at Trent Maxwell, the middle-aged owner of the dry cleaners and laundry service in town, who sat in the table next to us.

I nodded, not wanting to talk about that place of horror.

"I figure you know stuff. You seem to be involved in all the murders around here."

Something snapped. I shot out of the booth, seized his coarse plaid shirt, and rammed it under his chin. My right hand was at my side, but clenched in a tight fist.

"I did not murder James Wilson or Sheila Ritter, you dumb hick," I snarled.

A large hand dropped gently onto my shoulder. A soft voice said, "He knows you didn't."

My mom placed her hand on my left arm; after a few moments, I released my grip. I could feel the presence of the other customers and heard their silence.

"Trent Maxwell, that was a stupid thing to say," said Beulah. "Apologize, now!"

"Miz Megan, I didn't say that right. I meant that you're so smart that you know everything. I didn't mean to offend you."

I looked up at Eldon Strumple, a retired Methodist minister. He nodded, but kept his hand on my shoulder. It's what James, my recently deceased neighbor, would have done. Sadness washed over me.

"It was a terrible thing to see," I said as I looked back at Trent. "You want to know about the Percival deaths. Some say it was a murder-suicide. My response is that maybe it is, maybe it isn't. The State Patrol is still investigating. And that's all I have to say."

I slid back into the booth, wondering at my burst of temper.

"He is a dumb hick, Best Friend," said Beulah. "But don't you let him bother you none." Then she turned to sneer at Trent.

"We need to talk," said Mom, "in your office, right after we eat."

"I'm coming," said Patty.

A half hour later, I shut my office door then told Mom and Patty that the suicide never happened and that it was a double murder. They stared at me in shock.

"Oh, Lordy, there's a murderer out there," said Patty. "No wonder you're on edge."

"And your purse is heavy—you're carrying your gun. Megan, you need to be careful," said Mom.

"Oh, I plan to be, but I am involved, at least indirectly. State Farm hired me to investigate whether the life insurance policy is valid. It's a fairly new policy, so the death benefit is void if the policyholder committed suicide. It's unlikely that either Val or Junior committed suicide, but it has to be ruled out. But you two need to keep all of that in confidence."

Glenda rang me to announce my appointment.

"Send her in," I said to Glenda then hung up. "Okay, I need both you to be discreet."

I opened the door to Celeste. She seemed surprised that I had company till I introduced my guests, who both stayed by the window. I sat down in one of the client chairs and she sat in the other.

"Now Celeste, you said you thought Fred Goblet was the killer. Why? That's a very serious charge."

"What does it matter? It was a suicide and a murder…everybody says so."

"Maybe not. The State Patrol is still investigating."

"Really?"

"So, what's with Fred?" I asked.

"Have you ever met him?"

"No, but I know Gabby. I handled her auto injury claim."

"There's an Abby, too," said Patty.

"Abby and Gabby?" asked Mom.

"Abigail and Gabriella," said Patty.

"And Dave and Shiny," said Celeste.

"No…someone named their child Shiny Goblet? You're kidding us," said Mom.

I chuckled. That did sound funny.

"Oh, that's Fred, the oily snake," said Celeste. "I forgot how he got that nickname. But he's sneaky and mean. That's why he's divorced. Who'd want to be married to him? Good thing he never had any kids. My mom is a Goblet, too. A cousin."

"Okay, so your mom has the four cousins—Abby and Gabby, who are twins, and then Fred and Dave," I said. "They all live in Kimball."

Celeste nodded.

"So why have I always heard about a feud between the Redmonds and the Goblets?" I asked.

"Oh, it's just talk as far as I know. But it's probably because Granny Goblet is the mother of both families."

"Should I be taking notes?" asked Mom with a smirk.

"I wish my mom was funny. Ah, so Lucille, we call her Granny, married Howard Redmond way back, had the four Redmond boys, but then divorced him because he was a mean drunk. Then she married Rusty and had Fred, Dave, Abby, and Gabby."

"No, no. Now you're telling us there's a Rusty Goblet?" asked my mom.

Celeste chuckled. "Well, it's Russell, but he's funny. He doesn't mind being called Rusty. Fred doesn't like Shiny. It makes him mad."

"Do you really think Fred is a murderer?" I asked.

"Oh, he could murder. Don't know if he did. I mean, why? The Percivals got along with the Goblets and the Redmonds, as far as I know."

"Who's Darold?" I asked.

"Darold? What a stupid name. I have no idea."

"How's Mitch?" I asked.

"Oh, it started out rough," said Celeste. "Didn't eat well, didn't drink well, which is bad 'cause his drugs are in his juice. Bit his wrist bloody. Got pretty agitated, but then calmed down when I gave him a new red ball. But he sleeps okay with Noah by his side." She smiled. "Noah said Mitch keeps trying to sleep on his pillow with him, so I don't think Noah sleeps well. Tonight, Noah's gonna try sleeping on two pillows so it's harder for Mitch to roll onto his pillow. Noah calls him the 'human heating pad' because he's so warm when he sleeps—heats up the whole bed."

I felt myself flushing warm with emotion so I went around my desk, opened a drawer, and then handed Celeste two chocolate bars.

"These are for your trouble," I said. "They're from Belgium."

"Oh, great. Are they from the Flemish or the Walloons?"

I laughed. "Sorry, I don't know." And this is for Mitch." I took a big plastic bag from the cabinet behind me and handed it to her.

She pulled out a big book of Vincent Van Gogh paintings.

"Mitch has always liked this painting," I said turning to the print of "Starry Night" on the wall behind me.

"Oh, I've heard of him," she leafing through the book. "Oh, yeah, he cut off his ear. I like this stuff, too. Mitch will like this because of the colors. We'll give it to him first thing after his snack when he gets home from school. I told my mom we should watch Wizard of Oz, you brought that from his house. Mitch loves it, even the brown part."

"I bet it's Judy Garland that he loves," said Mom.

"How did you know?" asked Celeste. "Oh, you're a mom, you know stuff. Yeah, Mitch loves singing women and girls...been in love with the Little Mermaid and Julie Andrews forever. Well, better go. Took the day off to help my mom sort through Mitch's stuff."

"I could probably get back in to get more stuff...like his dresser," I said.

"Really, you could?"

"I'm dating a guy in the State Patrol."

"Oh, that big guy I saw at the jail?"

"No, he's married...this is another guy. Ask your mom and let me know."

"Okay. Hey your receptionist makes really good pastries."

"That's Glenda the Good Witch of the North."

She laughed as she shoved the chocolate bars in her purse then stood with the book pressed against her side.

Patty opened the door for her.

"Thanks for this stuff," Celeste said as she left.

Patty closed the door behind her.

"You bought that book for Davey, didn't you?" asked Mom.

I nodded. Davey was a higher functioning autistic, a walking encyclopedia of baseball statistics who worked at Custer's before he was murdered. Now, I was beginning to feel increasingly concerned and protective of Mitch. Oh, someone said something. I looked up. My mom was standing beside me. She gave me a kiss on the cheek.

"We'll see you tonight," she said.

Chapter 5

AFTER work, I went to sit in my Fort, a small hut built on top of Big Leo for me in the winter months. A double murder, Lord above. I should wait and let the State Patrol investigate and make their announcement. Then I could simply write a report for State Farm based on their conclusions and recommend extension of benefits to Mitch and Darold, whoever he was. Maybe Uncle Bill would know him. Yeah, that's what I should do—just keep my distance from it, forget what I saw, what I figured out. Oh, yeah, the law firm files, they could get subpoenaed. I hated the thought of losing those files without knowing what was in them. Well, I should do something about that then maybe this haunting, foreboding itch would disappear like an old rash.

I wanted to act on the files without a crowd, so I took my phone from my coat and called Derek, my childhood friend, who now lived next door in the Wilson family house. Derek moved back home with his wife, Tina, after his father, James, suffered a stroke. James, who had been like a father to me amid the coldness of my own father, died last month. That wound was still raw. Vonny, the daughter, lived in Denver. Derek was a computer nerd who worked from home for a Scottsbluff computer security company. He answered right away and confirmed he was coming for dinner. He said he could get the equipment I needed and could install it tomorrow. He was loaded with questions, but I put him off and requested he not mention this conversation tonight.

Before I went back to the house, I walked to the western edge of the bluff to listen. They came to me—Mr. and

Mrs. Wilson, James and Beverly—in their low, soothing tones, never words, just sounds, the ones I'd heard since I was young. First it had been my twin brother Scott, whom I didn't recall; then there was the wailing woman I probably imagined was my mother. But I heard Scott, all those miles away in Omaha. Now I heard both James and Beverly, just as James had heard Beverly, and Lew listened to his mother. We were the only three that heard the voices in the wind—that I knew of. Maybe others heard in another place, in another stretch of this rugged land of bluffs, buttes, gullies, and buffalo grass. I would never know, for I wasn't likely to go asking around—people already thought I was weird.

Back in the house, Patty roasted chicken while I stewed over my plans and the information I would divulge to the group. During supper, we avoided the gruesome topic; though it was on everybody's mind. As soon as we were all assembled in the family room and sipping our bourbon, the discussion started.

"I just can't believe Junior would kill Val or himself…it doesn't make sense," said Bill.

"Everybody is saying that," said Derek, a tall African American with a square head and a pink lower lip.

"It doesn't make sense because it didn't happen," said Jay, who took a seat next to me on the sofa.

"What?" said Bill. "Val was shot in the head and Junior died from a bullet to his head with his own rifle. That's what I heard."

"All that's true. But Megan figured out that what we saw was what we were meant to see, and that it's actually a double murder," said Jay.

"Megan figured it out…why doesn't that surprise me?" said Tina.

"You or any good cop would have spotted it. And I was slow to understand it. Now I wish I could get it out of my head."

"Several cops missed a clue I won't discuss," said Jay. "A great deal of forensic analysis must be completed before an official announcement is made.'

"But this is torturing people," said Bill.

"What we need is a good rumor for people to grab on-to." I said. "Would you object to that?"

"No, as long as it's unofficial," Jay said.

"Well, I know how to take care of that." I glanced over at several grinning faces as I waited for her to answer the phone. "Hi, Best Friend. I just have something to say real quick that you can tell anyone you like." I chuckled at Beulah's cheeky response. "Yes, I know you're the one for the job. So, about Junior and Val, just say it was probably not a murder-suicide, but the police won't confirm that till they're done with all the tests they do."

Jay nodded.

"Yeah, it was hard to believe. But say it's not clear, but that Junior and Val are the people we always thought they were." I paused. "Yes, a collection for Mitch would be a great idea. Call Jeff Finch in the morning. The bank knows how to set up a fund. Okay, I'll see you tomorrow. Good-night."

I shoved my phone in my back pocket.

"I bet she was pleased to hear it," said Mom.

"Oh, she's tickled. And she'll be on the phone till late then tomorrow she'll tell everyone who passes through the diner's doors the news."

"But there's a murderer loose," said Mom.

A damn smart one to fool some cops—that eliminated several scoundrels I knew.

"But why did they get murdered?" asked Bill. "They wouldn't own anything to steal."

"Why do people kill?" mused Patty. "Revenge, mon-ey…was either of them having an affair?"

"I don't believe that for a minute," said Bill. "They were good Christian folks devoted to each other and to

Mitch. Did you know he was actually their second child? They had a boy who died just after birth with a bad heart."

"That scene didn't look like a crime of passion was committed—it looked like cold calculation, premeditation," I said.

"What about money?" asked Mom. "I'd only met them once."

"Junior worked at Smokey's and Val at Shaver's...so no...they were doing okay, but not rich, far from it," said Bill.

"I'm the personal representative...the executor of the estate, so I'll be finding out about their finances. Now this is in strict confidence...but I'll only mention it because I have a question...but Val had a life insurance policy. The beneficiaries would be Mitch and Darold. That's the question—who is Darold?"

"He's a Redmond and Val's brother," said Patty. "Celeste didn't recognize the name because he's always been called Buster."

"And he'll be coming into some money," said Derek. "Did he kill them for the money?"

"So who's Celeste?" asked Tina.

"The niece of Val and Junior, and a former jail mate of mine," I said.

"Okay, now what's the deal with these Redmonds?" asked Mom.

"Howard Redmond, who was half Lakota, married Lucy...Lucille," said Patty. "They had four sons...I was once married to the youngest, Greg, who now lives in North Platte and works for Union Pacific."

"Oh, that's right," I said. "My dad helped you with the divorce." I looked over to Bill.

"Yeah, and I punched Greg's lights out. Anyway, Patty, go on."

"So Howard and Lucy had four sons, Gary, Gage, Grant, and Greg. Gage and Grant work for an electrician in Kimball. They're all in their fifties."

"Where's Gary?" asked Jay, who was typing notes into his smart phone.

"He died in Vietnam," said Bill. "It crushed them, especially Howard."

Patty nodded. "Now Howard was known as a mean, abusive drunk, so Lucy divorced him and later married Russell Goblet, who's a nice man…er…well, he's in a home in Kimball with Alzheimer's now. Their kids are Abby, Gabby, Fred, and Dave. Howard later remarried. Pearl is a toughie. Story has it the first time Howard hit her, she hit him over the head with a shovel and then promised to do it in his sleep every time he hit her or the kids."

"Who were—?" I asked.

"Valerie and Darold," said Patty.

"So who's still alive besides Russell?"

"Well, Howard always had a bad heart, so he's been gone a long time. But Pearl and Granny Goblet—Lucy—are still alive and kicking."

"How old is Mitch?" asked Tina. "He shares the life insurance with Buster, right?"

"Mitch is the sweetest, purest soul who ever lived, next to Davey," I said. "Mitch is profoundly autistic, mentally retarded and, nonverbal. Val used to say he was fifteen going on two."

"But now worth some money, so somebody to be protected," said Tina.

I nodded.

"Megan, is it a big policy?" asked Patty.

"Not big, but maybe large to some people. It will certainly help Mitch's aunt and uncle, Helen and Kenny Percival—they'll be taking custody of him."

"What do we know about Buster?" asked my mom.

Patty shook her head. "Not much. I haven't seen him in years. He'd be tall and lean like all Redmond men. He's only a quarter Indian, but has dark hair and would be about forty. I've never seen him in Dexter, though Val said he used to visit."

"You'll never confuse a Goblet with a Redmond—the Goblets are short and stocky like Rusty, with light brown hair," said Bill. "They look like Hobbits."

That lightened the mood enough that root beer floats became the entertainment. The gang milled about with their desserts, scooping, slurping, and chatting. For a few minutes, Jay, Mom, and I were alone in the kitchen. Mom plopped the last dollop of vanilla ice cream into the tall glass and I filled it with root beer then handed it to Jay, who followed me down the hall.

"I've already got background checks going on the Percivals," said Jay. "You know Marty Loske, she's really good with those. With this so-called feud between the Redmonds and the Goblets, they'll all be included. I haven't heard of anything except tough talk and a few bar fights between the men, so it's hardly the Hatfields and the McCoys."

"You did well tonight," I said to him.

"What? I hardly said anything."

"Right. This was a time to listen. There were plenty of smart people in the room who knew what questions to ask. And now you understand who knows the most about these families, at least in this little group. And they know a lot more, though Bill and Patty may not understand what's important."

"Your friend Beulah would know these families."

"Oh, there's a lot of people who do. And we need to find Darold 'Buster' Redmond. We know he'll benefit from the life insurance, but is he smart enough to commit those murders?"

In time, the house cleared and Jay and I heated up my bedroom sheets. Later, I lay against his side, admiring how the fireplace cast a glow over his body. Just as I was ready to turn my admiration into more action, he turned to me.

"You should come to my gym. We can bring guests."

"But I have a treadmill and I just bought that weight bench. I can get bigger weights for you to use."

"You don't get it. I want to show you off...and that's the straight-up truth."

"Oh...um...I don't own any skimpy spandex."

He smiled. "Showing off is a big deal to guys. And you are—"

"The Goddess of Kick-Ass. Yeah, I've heard."

"I was going to say my gorgeous babe. And yeah, you do have a certain reputation. Dating you makes me look like a stud."

I ran my fingers down from his chest to his responsive man-parts. "You are a stud. Why do other people need to know? I consider myself privileged that I know you have Mr. Majestic here...just for me."

"I will say you don't have the biggest anything I've ever seen. You bring a hunk of wood to the movies because your shrimpy little legs can't reach the floor. C'mon."

I laughed, duly accused.

"Well, your guts...those are big...in the figurative sense."

I smiled. "Oh, my small intestines stretch for miles."

He rolled me on my back and kissed my belly. "I love these guts, these arms, these short little legs. I love every inch of you." He brought his face to mine. "I love you."

That caught my breath.

"Don't say anything. I think maybe it scares you. So just relax. I don't mean to push."

He dropped his head into my neck, giving me a chance to quiet my pounding heart. Love. Was I ready for that?

In the morning, I feigned sleep when Jay rose. He said he loved me. My blood pressure jolted and launched upward. Breathe, relax, think, breathe deeper. I joined him in the shower. At breakfast, I steered the conversation back to murder or at least the scene.

"In time, I'll need to sell the Percival house, but it would be hard to sell with the north addition unfinished," I said. "Could Hank and Lew start work again if they stay out of the rest of the house?"

"They wouldn't have a bathroom," he replied.

"Oh, they'll figure that out. The door has a lock. It was probably meant to keep Mitch from wandering in there. Did you notice all the doors in the house had locks?"

"Um…yeah. We can chain the door locked."

"Oh, and I should get the food out of the fridge and cupboards," I said.

"We can arrange for you to go out there when we have a trooper there."

"Oh, yeah. I'm supposed to get Mitch's dresser."

He nodded and was quiet. Finally, he put down his toast and said, "So you never said if you'd come to the gym."

"Oh, sure I will…as long as it's on the weekend."

He smiled and gave me a kiss.

"Mmm. Strawberry jelly. But really now, I don't have anything tight and stretchy. That's not me."

"Well, you look best naked, but that won't do. Just a T-shirt and sweat pants will work."

Late in the morning, Derek arrived at the office with the new equipment. Yesterday, I'd asked Brian and Gus to move the massive oak desk into the basement storage room. It contained rows of old cabinets for my dad and his partner's old files that I now kept as custodian. I wanted to start scanning old files into documents, so this would kick-start that process. As Derek set up the scanner and the new laptop, I opened the fireproof cabinet that held the Goblet, Percival, and Redmond files.

"Now these are the files I need scanned into this laptop," I said to Mom. "The Wi-Fi connection has been disabled, so it should be secure. We'll set a password for entry. These files are the only ones to be scanned into this laptop. If you need to leave the room, lock it. This is top secret stuff. So don't discuss it with anyone, not even anyone in the office. I don't know what's in them, but I don't want the State Patrol to seize these without having access to the contents."

"Does Jay know about this?" she asked.

"Hmm. Guess I forgot to mention it. We three are the only ones who know about this. Let's keep it that way."

"Why do I feel like Nancy Drew's mother? Oh, Derek, how's Barnaby?" asked Mom.

"He still needs a doggy shrink. Tina's trying to be a good sport, but last night he peed on our hearth."

"That's terrible," I said, laughing. "No really, the poor pooch."

"Yeah, he spends a lot of time outside. He misses my dad. I don't know how to fix that."

"What about another dog for company?" said Mom. "Maybe a puppy to give him lots of trouble. It might work as a distraction."

"Well, he would need to be house-trained. I'm tired of mopping up doggy grief. The house smells like a nursing home—disinfectant and urine." He flipped on the switch and the scanner-copier lit up and hummed. "I think you're ready."

"Well, sorry, Mom. I feel like I'm locking you in a dungeon. Here are the keys. Derek, send me a bill."

"Will do. Okay, I'm off. Hey, did you know Beulah called up Tina for help? I don't think she liked Blaine's ideas on fixing up the diner. Said she needed a smart woman's advice. I guess somebody told her Tina has a business degree. See ya."

After he left, I told Mom we were meeting Celeste for lunch.

"Do you really trust everything she says?" she asked.

"Not a chance. But exaggeration can be revealing. After a fair amount of chocolate and lot of small talk, she confessed she's dating Dave Goblet's son, Caleb. Fred always talks against her to Dave, so she says. But she still claims Shiny Fred had been feuding with Junior. It's hard to know what to think, but I'll get to the bottom of it."

"And she's a good way to keep tabs on Mitch," she said.

Later in the day, I got a call back from Lew. He was pleased they would get to finish the work in the Percival house. He even agreed to haul Mitch's dresser to Sidney. I expected a blow up anytime with Kenny and Helen. I'd already made arrangements with Smokey to receive Junior's paycheck and with Shaver's to obtain Val's. Melanie filed a request with the post office for Percival mail to be sent to Docket Law. I'd even warned my staff to expect an angry visit by them, but they weren't to be admitted in the building without an appointment. I wanted to be ready for them.

Chapter 6

SATURDAY afternoon, I lay on the sofa watching a Husker game. Uncle Bill lounged in the recliner with a beer in his hand. Mom and Patty were shopping somewhere, a task I preferred to do at my computer. I shopped like a guy—if I was at a mall, I parked near my destination, went into the specified store, bought the item, and then left. I didn't like the slow walking and the look at this and look at that mentality. I'd much rather hang out with my uncle. Then just as our offense was driving, my phone buzzed. It was Lew, which made me sit up with a jolt. His message got me off the sofa and into Bill's concerned gaze.

"I need to go to the Percival house," I said. "I'm sure I'll be back soon."

"Anything wrong?" Bill asked.

"Well, they found something peculiar at the Percival house."

"Do you want me to come with you?"

"No, that's okay. There's a cop in the other part of the house, but you know how Lew and Hank are with cops."

Instead of parking out front, I drove to the broken up black top alley behind the house. The alley appeared to be rarely used, except to store garbage cans. In fact, most people didn't even have gates to the alley through their fences. Many people had installed six-foot fences along their backyards either for privacy or for containing larger dogs. The Percival yard included such a fence—probably to restrain Mitch, who had a history of bolting.

I entered through the rear gate of the fence and walked along the side away from the sidewalk and the oak tree, though the ground along the sidewalk was now well-trampled. Just before I knocked on the back door, I saw through the window that Lew and Hank stood in the middle of the room, staring at the floor. Their sense of alarm prevented them from working. They both jerked when I knocked. Lew scurried over to let me in.

"Oh, Miz Megan! It's not ours, I swear!" blurted Lew.

"What are you talking about? Now relax and tell me."

"Me and uncle don't smoke, but there they are."

I followed him to where Hank was staring. On the floor lay a white matchbook.

"Megan, that was never here before," said Hank. "Like Lew said, we don't smoke. I useta enjoy a cigar now and then, but Linda won't let 'em in the house."

I bent down to look at them. In bright green writing the cover read "The Green Onion, Kimball, NE."

"Have either of you touched them?" I asked.

"Nope, know better than that," said Hank.

"Did you tell the trooper in the other part of the house?"

"Nope, we wanted to wait for you."

I photographed the book of matches with my phone then knocked on the glass-paned door that led to the rest of the house. Recognizing the approaching officer, I gave Loske a wave. His wife worked for the Sidney police; I met her when I was in jail.

"Good afternoon, Officer Loske. Lew and Hank summoned me to look at something they'd found in this room." I pointed to the book of matches.

Loske was forties like his wife and also sandy-haired. He photographed the matchbox then stood.

"And you say neither of you had seen this before?"

"No, sir," said Hank. "We woulda seen it because we just put up this section of drywall last week. And like I told Megan here, we don't smoke. I never been to that bar. Don't usually go to Kimball."

Loske looked at Lew, who was herky-jerky with nerves. "No, not ours Mr. Officer."

"Thank you, I'll be right back."

When Loske left the room, I tried to give Hank and especially Lew my most reassuring nods. Loske returned with tweezers and a plastic bag. He turned the matchbook over, which indicated the same logo as the front side. He photographed it then put it in the plastic bag with the tweezers.

"Who was the electrician here?" I asked.

"Gage Goblet from Werner Electric in Kimball," said Hank. "Grant came a couple of times. But I never seen them smoke."

"I wonder if he's been back here?" I mused.

"I don't know why," said Hank. "He finished his work on them sockets by lunchtime on the day of the murders. Then he left and didn't come back in the afternoon. We left about four and didn't even see Mr. or Mrs. Percival. They asked us if we'd start after eight-thirty and leave by four so we didn't disturb Mitch, their son."

Loske walked over to inspect the back lock as he dialed his phone.

"It was locked when we came this morning," said Hank. "Megan gave us the key."

Loske nodded to him then turned away.

"I'm the executor for the estate," I said. "I'm starting to think new locks on this house would be a good idea. Who knows how many people have received keys to this house over the years."

Kenny and Helen would've had access to this house, but I kept that to myself.

"Did Gage Goblet have a key to the house?" I asked.

"Yeah, he did," said Hank. "Never saw that he left it when he was done. We would have seen that. We gave our key to Officer McNeill when she came to interview us."

I started walking around the room, acting like I was inspecting the work, but something was eating at me—more than the book of matches. Danger? Maybe not that strong, but something. The ladder that had been outside on the day of the murders was set against the east wall, so it belonged to Hank or Lew, not Junior.

"By the way, Sergeant Merritt is on his way," said Loske. "I'm going back in the front room so you guys can go back to work. Megan, you can join me, if you wish."

"I will, but first I want to discuss the ceiling with my workers."

As soon as Loske left, Hank asked, "Don't you like it, Megan? Mr. Percival said he wanted a drop ceiling."

"Oh, that's fine work. I just said that so he'd leave. So do you guys have any guesses or um, feelings on who the killer was? You said murders earlier, so you know it wasn't suicide."

Hank shook his head. "That's what we heard at Custer's. I don't know these folks super good, but they seemed real nice, ya know, hard working. We were here at the same time sometimes, and I never even heard them argue."

"Lew, any ideas?"

"No, Megan. I don't see how anybody coulda been here, except later when Mr. Kenny came. But we were already gone."

"Could Gage Goblet have come back?" I asked.

"Well, ah, he still had a key, I guess. But why? He'd finished his work and cleared all his stuff out. There wasn't nothin' for him to do."

"Megan," said Hank, "Officer McNeill came to talk to us. Didn't act like she thought we done it. But she said nobody was seen coming to the house except Kenny. And she asked us like you, what or who, but we don't know. Can't wrap my head around it."

"Lew, I haven't seen you come over to walk on my land, I mean, by my house. Can you hear at your house?"

He nodded. "I can. I can hear my mom there, too, and I don't have to walk far. The truth is…ah... I don't want to be botherin' Mr. Derek or his nice wife. They been through enough."

"Lew, do you feel?"

"Megan, I know what you're meanin' and um…it's…hard to…ya know…say exactly."

"Do you feel anything here? Now that the cop and the matches are gone."

"Just that I'll feel glad to get away from a house where there were two murders. I know what you're getting' at. You knew your dad had a heart attack from two streets away and I heard you felt it when James had his stroke. But…I just don't feel that stuff."

"Did you know when your mom had died?"

"No, Salt had to tell me."

Now I was feeling stupid for asking. I looked away from their faces; I was in a weirdo class of my own.

"Um, can I ask you, Megan, are you feeling something here?" asked Hank.

"I can hear Junior's surprise and his grunt, and I hear Val screaming. I'm not looking forward to going back into those rooms. Okay, and I'll tell you something else, but you both need to promise not to tell anyone. After I came to the scene, when the bodies were still here, I…ah…felt danger when I walked into this room."

"This room?" asked Hank. "Danger. Hmm."

I nodded. "Does that make any sense to you guys at all?"

"I'll think on it," said Lew. "Do you feel it now?"

I shook my head. "Anyway, do you guys know the flooring intended?"

"Carpet, but it's on back order," said Hank. "We'll install that and then we do the baseboards."

"A company from Kimball is putting in a gas fireplace," said Lew. "Should be nice…not fancy like yours. Be about a foot and a half deep with ceramic tile in front. We built out this box another foot. We covered the front with plywood because there's no insulation behind it."

"By the way, what did you think of Gage and Grant Goblet?" I asked.

Lew shrugged.

"Do they do good work?"

"Yeah, they do," said Hank. "But you want to know more than that."

I smiled.

"Gage was okay. Kinda smart-alecky. Liked to make jokes that he thought we wouldn't understand. Sometimes I didn't. He liked actin' smarter than us. Grant hardly ever said a word."

"I didn't understand what Gage was sayin' most of the time," said Lew. "But, yeah, good workers. Got nothin' against them. Grant was real quiet. Liked him better."

"Did either man seem threatening?"

Lew and Hank looked at one another then shook their heads.

"Gage is just a smart-ass," said Hank. "Oh, and we made arrangements with Helen Percival," said Hank. "We're taking the dresser out to Sidney when we're done. But I don't know if the policeman knows it."

"I'll go talk to him. Maybe you guys and Linda would like to come over some night for poker and bourbon."

"Oh, we'd like that," said Lew.

I smiled and went through the door, closing it behind me. Officer Loske was standing with Sergeant Merritt in the TV room. I was glad I didn't need to go into the kitchen or front room. I asked permission for Mitch's dresser to be taken to him. Merritt consented.

"And no, nothing on the forensic results," said Merritt.

"Anything on their computer?" I asked.

"No, but you know I shouldn't tell you if there was," said Merritt with a smile. "Junior liked to look at pictures of exotic trees. And they do some shopping online. And emails to friends were about it. Oh, a spreadsheet for their checking account. So, nothing there."

"So we have a double murder where nobody is seen coming and going at the time when the murders are committed, except for Kenny," I said.

"I interviewed him," said Merritt. "I didn't get the impression that he, well, this took some brains, and he might not fit the profile. And he didn't seem to understand about how Val died. He said he needed to phone her at Shaver's. He's excitable, but not wily."

"And why would he kill them?" said Loske. "The motive is a problem. From what we've heard, the brothers got along. Plus, now they've got the son, Mitch, to deal with."

"There is a life insurance policy," I said. "I'm officially representing State Farm. And no, I'm not authorized to divulge the value of the death benefit...though it would be substantial to most people. It's a policy issued less than two years ago, so suicide would nullify the benefits."

"Who are the beneficiaries?" asked Loske.

"It's a policy on Val, so Junior was the primary beneficiary...he's out...so the money would go to Mitch and Val's brother Darold, commonly referred to as Buster. We haven't heard from him yet, though I bet you've started looking for him." I glanced at Merritt. "So nothing on fingerprints or the blood stain yet?" I asked.

"Nothing conclusive," Merritt said.

"Did anyone in the neighborhood hear the gunshot?" I asked.

"Ruth Sempole said she heard a pop or a sharp crack, but thought it was a TV. She's the one who saw the Eldritch men leave before Val and Junior arrived. And she also said no other vehicle was around till Kenny came. Kenny called the police when he saw Junior. Chief Tate was the first on the scene, here within a couple of minutes, and then a county deputy arrived," said Merritt. "Kenny was kneeling on the floor next to his brother."

"Was the Percival TV on when Chief Tate arrived?" I asked.

"Yes, the TV in the front room was on. Tate said it was some police show or movie he didn't recognize."

"Maybe the killer was trying to drown out the sound of the gun."

"Now here's the bizarre thing…and this is in strict confidence…the rifle used to kill Junior Percival was owned by Kenny Percival."

I stared at Merritt for a moment.

"Junior Percival kept a small armory in his basement," said Merritt.

"What kind of guns did he have?" I asked.

"All hunting rifles, nothing automatic, and no handguns. Oh, and he had some knives, too, all the kind of stuff a hunter would own. He had fishing rods and gear, too."

"How many rifles were there?"

"Six rifles in the basement, and four knives."

"Did he keep any weapons on the main floor?"

"No."

"So Kenny wasn't concerned about his safety," I mused. "If he knew of a threat, he would have kept one of his own guns where he had easy access to it."

"And no guns in his truck. Now Megan, I've told you information that must be kept in strict confidence."

"Though I can tell my boyfriend."

Both men chuckled.

"When do you plan to announce that it was a double murder? I know there are rumors going around about both a murder-suicide and a double murder."

"That's up to Lieutenant Young, but I doubt he announces it until all the tests are complete."

"Well, I won't send my report to the insurance company until I absolutely need to. If Val and Junior were murdered for the life insurance money, I don't want the insurer to start passing out that money…especially to someone like Mitch."

Chapter 7

ON Sunday, Jay came to church with me then came back for dinner at Mom's. I think he was concerned that I'd back out of going to the gym with him. We stayed to watch the Cowboys and Giants play and to digest. At my house, I showed Jay the clothes I planned to wear to his Sidney gym. It was a simple navy sweat suit with a bright blue Creighton T-shirt.

"See, no spandex," I said. "It wouldn't be right for me to look like a bint. I might see clients of mine. They want to respect my abilities, so it's better for them to see my petitions than my abs."

"I love your abs," he said, "but I don't want to share the view. Still, your knife scar makes you look tough. Both your uncle and mom say you lived when you really should've died."

"Oh, don't get me thinking about that. Let's go."

At the fitness center, the clerk at the front desk called Jay "Lieutenant."

"Do people often call you by your rank?" I asked as we walked toward the weight room.

"Oh, sometimes. Do people call you the 'Pocket Docket'?"

"No, I've grown taller."

Jay chuckled. "You haven't asked, but I know about the book of matches."

"I assumed you did."

"And Merritt told me all that he told you. He thinks it's important to keep you informed...says you figure out things."

"Well, if I do, don't tell anyone…I'm not looking for trouble. Hey, do you know those two guys over by that far bench?" I asked as I led him toward the young men.

"No, who are they?"

"Mitch's cousins, brothers now for practical purposes. I'll introduce you then you should skedaddle. I want to talk to them."

"I'll do my best skedaddling. Who says that?"

"I do, starting today. Hey, guys. I'm Megan. I saw you at your house."

"Oh, we know who you are…everybody does."

"Ah, great. This is Lieutenant Jay Young with the State Patrol."

Jay shook their hands.

"I'm gonna start stretching," said Jay. He walked over and sat down on a mat.

"How's Mitch doing?" I asked.

"Pretty good," said Ryan, the high school senior.

"I bet it's thrown your house upside down just when you want to be thinking about your aunt and uncle."

"Yeah."

"Did you know Davey Shuster?" I asked. "Man, when things went wrong for him, he could start a bloody brawl. He gave Brian Culhane all he could handle, but Brian knew to hang on even when he was getting pummeled."

"Mitch hasn't been that bad," said Noah, the younger brother. "To calm down, Mitch likes to walk around the house or bounce in his chair. I try to take him for walks, but he doesn't like the cold wind. When he gets really upset, he hits his head on the wall…busted in the drywall a couple of times."

"He likes Baxter, that's our old basset hound," said Ryan.

The brothers looked at each other and chuckled.

"Mitch decided he wants Baxter with him when he sits in his special chair," said Ryan. "So he goes and finds Baxter and carries him to the chair and puts him on his feet.

Baxter doesn't like being carried under his armpits and I don't blame him, but he was smart enough to stay with Mitch for a while. Then the next day, Mitch did the same thing. And Baxter stayed with him."

"So today, before we came here, Mitch went looking for Baxter, but Baxter saw him coming," Noah said with a laugh. "Baxter sprinted to Mitch's chair and waited for him. When Mitch sat down, Baxter laid across his feet. Mitch made a funny squeal then Baxter just went to sleep. They were like that when we left."

"That's a hoot," I said. "My neighbor and friend Kayla Ritter goes and helps in the special ed room at school."

"I've seen her," said Ryan. "She's the one whose Mom parked her car on the railroad tracks then the train killed her."

"That's technically correct, but it was really meth that killed her," I said.

"Kayla's pretty," said Noah.

"True, but she's not dating age yet. And she's still grieving the loss of her mother. It takes time. You'll see. You'll be grieving your aunt and uncle for a long time and adjusting to Mitch will be an even longer ordeal."

"He can be fun," said Ryan.

"And difficult," I said.

The guys nodded.

"We have to use bicycle combination locks on the fridge and the cupboards with food or he steals it," said Noah.

"Barb Shuster told me that they did that, too. And she had to hide her favorite snacks in pots and pans."

"We should try that," said Ryan.

"I'm sure you'll figure out lots of things. Barb told me the toughest times were when they forgot to keep their sense of humor about stuff Davey did."

They nodded. In tank tops and shorts, neither brother was big, but they were ripped, their muscles and body hair visible.

"I think Mitch is lucky to have you guys."

"And Celeste," said Noah. "When Mitch gets sleepy, he gathers pillows to burrow under and he tries to gather Celeste, too, like she's warm nesting material. She's a good sport, even when he wiggles his fingers into her hair."

"My dad doesn't know what to do with Mitch, but he tries to be patient," said Ryan. "We taught the two of them how to shake hands and high five each other."

"Well, that's good," I said. "Some autistics can't stand to be touched."

"Noise is his problem, and he doesn't like to be startled," said Noah.

"We know he's going to be with us from now on," said Ryan.

"And his family's money will come his way, but it's a slow process. Your folks will think it's too slow. The thing is…it will be triple slow because of Mitch' disability. This is a sad, hard, stressful time. But I'm the one to get the necessary things done…the attorney on record so everything goes through me. So I'm sure I'll be talking to your folks soon."

After I left the brothers, I found Jay doing bench presses with Merritt and two other guys I didn't recognize. Jay introduced me to them. They looked to be young cops, brown-nosing the bosses.

"Wanna try?" asked Jay as he let the weights clang into position.

"Nah, I don't like to show off in public," I said.

"Are you packin'?" asked one of the guys with a smirk.

I looked down at my sweat pants and T-shirt and said, "Not at the moment."

"It's a Glock, isn't it? Is it in your purse?"

"Are you packin' a search warrant, officer?"

As he and the other guy laughed, I greeted Merritt then turned to Jay.

"I'm heading for the nautilus equipment."

I turned and left, but I heard the cop say, "Ah, c'mon, let's see it."

I kept walking, unwilling to be annoyed by some green trooper.

A sharp voice said, "Shut up, shithead. Show some respect. How many murders have you solved? Why don't you two twerps go someplace else?"

Glancing back at Merritt, I gave him a nod then walked on.

On the way home, Jay asked, "Are you annoyed that I didn't stick up for you?"

"Heck no. They weren't worth your time...or mine. Merritt stepped in so his boss didn't need to act snarky. He's decided to play big brother to me."

"He has that complex. I heard some guy said something pretty mild to Tina, I think just to rile Derek. Merritt chucked him out the front door."

"Good for him."

"So what do you think about Kenny Percival owning the murder weapon?" Jay asked.

"I know it looks bad for him, but it just doesn't fit somehow. Merritt said there were six rifles in Junior's storage rack. Did Junior own all of them?"

Jay smiled. "Interesting question. And the answer is no. The case had room for eight rifles. Junior owned four, Kenny owned two. And in an interview today, Kenny said one of the knives was his, too. He said he stores his rifles in Junior's case because they hunt together."

"Hmm. Who needs four rifles?"

"Junior was an aspiring collector. Two of the rifles were antiques, Winchesters. Kenny says the other two rifles are used by his sons. Kenny said he had three rifles in the case at Junior's house."

"Makes sense," I said. "Both Junior and Kenny have come out to view my collection of Civil War guns and such at the firm. Junior nearly split a gut when I allowed him to take one of the rifles apart, clean it, and reassemble it. So, did someone break into the case?"

"No, it was locked and the key was just where Kenny said it would be. I had Rachel interview him with Detective Moore in the background. Kenny is easily riled, but she kept him calm," said Jay.

"Well, with guys, the testosterone gets bouncing back and forth, and then things can get out of control. But some people just know how to help people relax in stressful situations. Dexter Deputy Bo Schnitzel is good at it. I bet Marty Loske would be, too. Hey, why is she wasted watching jailbirds?"

"She does a lot of background checks. And she's there by necessity. She was State Patrol years ago, but her cruiser got rammed by some redneck. She has some nerve damage in her left hand from a nasty fracture."

"That's a lousy deal, but she is good with those vermin jailbirds," I said.

He laughed—he had great resonance when he really let loose. And I loved his smell, though it was a bit powerful at the moment with the closed windows and the heat on in his pickup. He brought his stuff for a shower at the gym, but he was probably hoping for an invitation to my shower, which I planned to offer. I loved his touch; the thought of him lathering me heated me more than my workout. I loved to touch him; it was hard to be near him and not want to press against him.

"Megan?"

"Oh, ah, yeah."

"So what do you think?"

"Oh, sorry. I was busy thinking about what I planned to do to you when we got back to my place. What did you say?"

"Never mind. I can't top that."

I chuckled when I felt the truck accelerate.

Although he was an excellent lover, his talking set him apart from any man I'd ever known. We could talk about anything and everything. We recently dared to venture into politics; I was pleased to discover another die-hard moderate. He seemed to enjoy my stories about traveling in Europe when I was in college, or maybe he was good at faking his attention. One topic did worry me—he'd started describing Christmas traditions at his house. Christmas was still a few weeks away, but I wondered if he would ask me to go to Omaha with him. Brian only had a dad and brother in Sidney, and I'd met them separately. This would be different, meeting the whole family in one big swoop—his parents, and his sisters and their families. My warm flush turned into sweaty panic. What would I say? I was probably safe for tonight—if he hadn't been thinking about sex before, my mentioning it would occupy his thoughts. He placed his hand on my thigh—nope, we wouldn't be talking about his family tonight.

The next morning, Melanie brought in a metal basket of correspondence.

"So there's nothing too interesting in the Percival mail, except for this," she said.

She handed me a letter from Aztec Mutual Life Insurance Company, a past due notice of the annual premium for Junior Percival's policy. The payment was late only thirty days, so a prompt payment would keep it in force. I raised my eyes to Melanie.

"Interesting is right. Looks like a bill to be paid. Take a look at this company, make sure they're legitimate. Get me the name and address of a supervisor to contact. Copy this page and give me the original and keep any information about this policy locked up. Thanks."

By early afternoon, I received the information I needed. I sent a check from Docket Law to pay the life insurance. In another letter, I advised the supervisor of the death of both Junior and Valerie Percival. I requested information on the policy and offered to represent their interests amid the murder investigation. By Thursday, I received the necessary information and a request to represent their company. I sent a letter back, agreeing to their terms.

Melanie came to the door. "Kenny Percival called a few minutes ago, spitting fire, so to speak. I said we'd be contacting him for an appointment."

He must have figured out he wasn't the executor of the estate. Things were getting worse for Kenny—with Junior's death, he along with Mitch were the beneficiaries of the Aztec life insurance policy. I walked over to the window to think through the facts—Kenny's rifle is the weapon that kills Junior, to which he had access; a murder scene where it didn't look like anyone else could have been the killer; and now he becomes the direct beneficiary along with Mitch of another twenty-five thousand each. Yes, it was looking worse by the moment for him. Why didn't I think he was the killer?

I asked Melanie to call Kenny and Helen to set up an appointment for tomorrow, at a time when Rich Dewey was available. Then I called Jack Sherman to change the locks on the Percival house. I sent a text to Jay advising him of the new security measure. After I sifted through the Percival mail, I packed up the secure laptop and left for the day. My first stop was the Cheyenne County Bank where I set up an account for the Percival estate. I deposited Junior and Val's paychecks into it and added my anonymous personal contribution to the fund set up for Mitch. Tomorrow would prove tumultuous. Melanie texted me, indicating the appointment was at eleven tomorrow. Then I met Jack Sherman at the Percival house. He put new locks on the exterior doors, disabled the garage door opener then changed that lock. I handed out keys to Hank and the State Patrol officer at the house with the understanding that we'd leave the outside storm doors unlocked. Then I went home to prepare.

Chapter 8

JUST before eleven, Kenny pounded on the front door. Glenda made him speak through the intercom before admitting him. He and Helen entered the office with Rich right behind them. I greeted them as Rich closed the door.

"Please have a seat," I said.

"The hell I will!" barked Kenny. "I go to collect Junior and Val's paychecks and find out you already have them. And how is it that you're the executor or the personal representative or whatever the hell that's called? My copy of my brother's will says I'm the executor."

"My copy of Val's will says I am," said Helen, who did sit down.

"I told them when I drafted the wills it would be better if they agreed on the executor. Later, they asked me to be executor. Gus, my partner, drafted a codicil for them. That's a supplement that adds or revokes the contents of their wills. Here is a copy of that codicil."

"Dammit, Megan, you crook!" said Kenny. "When was it written?"

"Right after Davey died." I opened a folder and extracted an envelope. "And here are two checks."

I set them on top of the codicil at the edge of my cherry wood desk directly in front of them.

"The check on your left is the amount of Junior and Val's last paychecks. On your right is a check in your names on behalf of Mitch. People in the area have contributed to a fund for him."

Kenny stared at the checks.

"Kenny, do you really think I'm going to steal money from Mitch?"

"People have given money to him? I didn't—" He looked down to examine the carpet.

"As personal representative, or executor, as most call it, I must also pay outstanding debts. I've already made some payments, here's a list of the bills I've paid. I'm keeping on the utilities at the house and I've authorized completion of the north addition they intended to build. It'll make selling the house much easier."

"They didn't plan to spend a ton on it," said Helen.

"I'm sticking to their original plans for the house. I'm getting all their financial records organized. I'll pay the bills, you take care of Mitch. Now, what information do you have on life insurance?"

"Junior had a policy giving life insurance to me and to Mitch…well, uh, after Val," he said. "It was for fifty grand."

"Total, so twenty-five to you and twenty-five to Mitch."

"But we'll be controlling his money, right?" said Helen.

"Yes, after we set up a Guardianship and a Conservatorship. There's a fair amount of paperwork with the county court and you both must attend a one-time training class."

"What the hell?" said Kenny. "What can they teach us about handling someone like Mitch?"

"Nothing, but you'll be filing annual reports with the state. Here's a schedule of the classes. It takes about two to three hours."

"That doesn't seem so bad if we only go once," said Helen.

"Now tell me, what do you know about Darold?"

"Who? Oh, Buster," said Kenny. "Haven't seen him for years. He's Val's brother."

"Then it makes sense that he and Mitch were named as secondary beneficiaries in Val's life insurance. Do you know how to contact him?"

"I didn't know she had a policy," said Helen. "But I'll look to see if I have a phone number or an address for him. How much is that policy?"

"Fifty thousand total, split equally. Now for the wills, because neither spouse survived the other, all assets, apart from the life insurance, go to Mitch. Both wills must be probated, that is, go through court, so you can sell the house with a clear title."

"Shit, sounds like a lot of paperwork," said Kenny.

"Right, lots of documents and filings all at a snail's pace. So if it seems slow, it's not me, I'll try to push it along. Like I said, I must pay the estate debts first, but I'll get money to you whenever I can. I know Mitch has expenses."

"I'm sorry, I thought you were being sneaky," said Kenny.

"No, just playing it by the book. But I will need cooperation from both of you," I said turning my gaze on Helen, who looked down.

"Kenny, time to sit down," said Rich.

Kenny plopped down into the chair.

"Now, we need to discuss the murders," I said. "Kenny, look at me. You've got things stacked against you. Rich will do all he can for you, but consider that you were the first one at the house and no other suspects have been identified. Junior was also killed with your rifle. And on top of it all, you benefit financially from the deaths."

Kenny lunged forward, but Rich was ready—he grabbed him from behind by the shoulders and pulled him back.

"Are you accusing me of the murders?"

I pressed a button on my desk phone.

"Sit down, now," I said.

The door opened and Chief Tate entered the room. "Kenny, sit down."

"Oh, so you called me here to get me arrested, you bitch."

"No, the Chief is here to keep you from clobbering me with my new floor globe. I'm just telling you how things stand."

Rich and Tate yanked Kenny back into the chair. I walked around the desk and stood in front of his chair. He looked up at me with a sneer, but I still didn't feel the danger I expected to feel with someone who killed two people.

"Kenny, I don't think you killed anyone," I said. "I can't say why, especially with your hot temper. But you need to be scared. You may or may not be arrested. The State Patrol is waiting on the results for a number of tests. This is the time for both of you to be calm, steady, and co-operative. You must think and exercise self-control—for each other and for your kids and Mitch. Be model citizens. Don't hide from people, just do what you normally would. And don't expect either insurance company to pay a cent until everything is resolved."

"You mean until they find the killer," said Helen.

I nodded.

"I see the way people have been looking at me," said Kenny.

I shrugged then walked back around to my desk chair.

"Don't assume you understand what they're thinking. Sure, some are wondering if you did it, but others are feeling sympathy for your loss. Since there's been no official announcement from the police, some people still wonder if it was a murder-suicide."

"That's wrong," said Kenny.

"I know. It was a double murder. And I know you've been interviewed extensively, but if you think of anything, you can call me, even if it's small or seems unimportant."

"But you'll go the cops," said Helen. "We know you're dating that State Patrol guy."

"Actually, he's the boss in this area. And I'll decide what I tell and to whom. Some secrets are meant to be kept. Plus, you have attorney-client privilege. I'm also the hired investigator for the two insurance companies."

"On what?" asked Kenny.

"Val's policy was relatively new, so suicide would void the policy. And on either life insurance claim, the murderer of the policy holder cannot collect insurance benefits according to state law."

"But I didn't kill anybody."

"Then who did?"

Kenny shook his head. "Shiny, I mean Fred Goblet and Junior had been arguing."

"About what? I asked.

"Man, how I wish I had asked him, but he never told me…maybe he was gonna. He usually tells me stuff."

I let silence hang in the room for a few moments.

"I know this is a terrible time for you. While the police are investigating, you can't even give them a proper service and burial to say goodbye. I'm so sorry."

Pain filled the room. Kenny and Helen lowered their eyes from me. Kenny's face was taut—not only had he lost his brother, he'd seen him after he was murdered, and now felt the sting of accusation.

"I saw your boys at the gym. They say Mitch uses Baxter as a foot blanket."

Slowly their faces changed from anguish to the sense of responsibility then to nodding confirmation. Kenny's face relaxed; then he smiled. He loved Mitch. That boy was safe with him. I studied him as he lifted his face to look at me. He didn't kill anyone.

"Maybe sometime you should bring Mitch out to my backyard. It was my childhood playground…it stretches for miles to the north, all the way to the interstate. One of the bluffs has a glassed-in hut you can sit in and see for miles."

Kenny nodded.

"Just remember, I'm on your side. And I'm going to do everything I can for Mitch."

A few minutes later, Melanie escorted them to the kitchen where Glenda would fill them with caffeine and sugar. Tate stayed in the office so it wouldn't look like he was following them.

Rich leaned against the wall grinning at me. "You played them like they were on strings, especially Kenny. Make him mad, then settle him down...make him sad then lighten his spirits. You're quite the puppeteer. You didn't learn that from your dad."

"I had a plan," I said.

Rich was right—my dad trained me, but my method of operation was different from his. My dad would have given them the facts and sent them on their way. I handled people in my own style, one that could get me in trouble if I wasn't careful. I'd toyed with Bert Bolger and he put a knife in me. This time I'd be more careful about how I investigated murder.

That afternoon, Jay called to tell me the forensic tests had been completed. So I arranged an impromptu gathering of Jay, Merritt, Rachel, and Tate at my house. Once the brandy and bourbon were distributed, Jay put on his glasses and held a few pages of paper in front of him as he sat on the sofa next to me.

"Now, what I think is interesting is the gun," Jay began. "It's a Ruger hunting rifle, a popular brand and model. The key to the case is kept nearby on a hook next to some tools on Junior's workbench, which isn't good security."

"Junior would've known all he needed to do was make it too difficult for Mitch to figure out," I said.

Jay nodded. "Now the fingerprints on the gun belong to Junior and Kenny. But there's also evidence of smudge marks on the barrel, as if the gun was also handled by someone wearing gloves. The fingerprint on the trigger is Junior's, but the killer could have pressed Junior's finger on the gun after Junior was dead. But here, the killer made a mistake. Junior is right-handed, the print on the trigger is from his left index finger."

"So, more evidence that this wasn't a suicide," said Rachel.

Jay nodded. "The bullet we pulled out of the wall was the correct ammo for the Ruger and the bullet fired from the rifle. So someone shoots Junior then goes after Val, who must have been standing nearby to get Junior's blood on her slipper. Val runs into the kitchen and is attacked. She couldn't kill Junior then herself because the gun is left by Kenny and she had bruises on her throat. We checked at Shaver's—she didn't have those earlier in the day according to co-workers. And she also has skin under her fingernails as if she tried to fight off the attacker. That skin is not Junior's."

"And Junior was surprised by the attack or he'd have put up a fight," said Merritt. "And we know Val was attacked because she screamed, though that evidence would not be admissible in court." He gave me a nod.

"Did Val have any other injuries?" I asked.

"She had a contusion on the back of her head," said Merritt.

"This is when she would be scratching the killer," said Rachel.

"I could have shot her at a distance of a few feet, but maybe the sick bastard was taunting her, so he gets in close before he shoots her." said Jay.

"Did you find the bullet that killed her?" I asked.

"Yes, in the bedroom because it went through the door. And yes, it was from the same Ruger rifle," said Jay.

"Why didn't the killer just choke her to avoid the noise?" I asked.

"Choking is much slower, despite what you see on TV," said Tate. "Val is tall and could put up some kind of fight. A struggle just leaves more evidence."

"My God, no wonder I felt such evil," I muttered.

"You said that the moment you stepped into the room...I heard you," said Tate. "Um, how—"

"I don't have an explanation, Chief," I said.

"Have you ever been wrong about your feelings?" he asked.

"No, but sometimes they're so vague."

"Are you a clairvoyant? I've heard about them."

I shrugged.

"You said something about danger when you were at the house," said Rachel.

"But I don't understand it. Ah, so what are we looking at in terms of a timeline," I asked, anxious to get out the line of inquiry.

Jay shuffled the papers and read: "Around eleven-thirty, the electrician leaves in his truck parked out front. He does not return. Lew and Hank leave for the day around three forty-five. At three-fifty, Junior came home. Kenny says his brother always comes home to shower after work before he goes to Sidney to pick up Mitch. Val came home at four-ten from Shaver's. No one is seen leaving the house. Helen calls Kenny at work at four forty-five to say no one has picked up Mitch and nobody is answering the phone at the house or on either cell phones. The cell phones confirm the missed calls. Kenny drives out to the Percival house from the root beer brewery, arriving at five till five. He calls emergency from his phone, which is confirmed, less than a minute later. Chief Tate arrives at four fifty-nine then a county deputy comes a couple minutes later."

"I got there right at five twenty," I said.

"And now we have the book of matches," said Merritt.

"As it turns out, it's the favorite watering hole of Fred "Shiny" Goblet," said Rachel. "He denies being in Dexter at the time of the murders, though he doesn't have a clear alibi. He says he was on the road, Highway 51, at the time. He says he went to meet a client, but the client wasn't there, so he was heading back to his office."

"Okay, wait," I said. "The Goblet brothers, Fred and Dave, own an independent insurance agency in Kimball. I wonder, do they sell life insurance for Aztec Mutual Life Insurance Company? That's the company for Junior's life insurance policy."

"I can find out," said Rachel.

"No, let me," I said. "I'm representing that company on the death benefits. I can find out without it looking like a police investigation. We don't want to alert anyone."

"What are you thinking?" asked Jay.

"That the killer is pretty smart, but he's made some mistakes because he's never done this before. So, okay. He sets up a scene to make it look like a murder-suicide, but as a backup, in case the police don't buy into the obvious, he tries to implicate Kenny by using his rifle and expecting him to be at the house. Then later he leaves a matchbook to throw in the possibility of Fred Goblet. The person who did this is familiar with the family and their routine. And somehow he knows about one or both of the life insurance policies. Again, that could implicate Fred or Dave Goblet. But again, this guy is smart, and it probably is a man, because he smashed Val's head into the door and she's a tall woman. Think about it—he manages to commit two murders, and then comes and goes from a house without being seen."

"And you've ruled out Kenny," said Jay.

"The police shouldn't, but I have, though I have no concrete evidence for it," I said. "But I think Junior and Val were killed for money, probably one or both life insurance policies."

I then summarized the insurance, the wills, and the beneficiaries for Junior and Val's estate.

"And the wills of both Val and Junior request that Kenny and Val become Mitch's guardian in the case they both die."

"In short, Mitch is the sole beneficiary of his parents' will, but the brothers, Kenny and Buster, stand to gain under the insurance policies," said Jay.

"Along with Mitch," I said.

"At some point this Buster will show up because people always do when money is involved," said Rachel. "So far, he's off the map—no tax return, no address, no employment record of any kind. So maybe he's a cash laborer somewhere in rural America. Nobody around here has seen him in several years."

"Are you ready to announce that the State Patrol believes these deaths to be a result of a double murder?" asked Tate.

"I am," said Jay.

"Will you be releasing the bodies for burial?" I asked. "Because a funeral may be just what we need to flush out Buster."

Chapter 9

AFTER Rachel and Merritt left, Jay and I cuddled together on the sofa to watch a movie. Jay was a film noir and Hitchcock junkie, but most of those seemed too heavy given the day's topic, so we settled on To Catch a Thief. Later, we created our own fireworks as the cold north wind rattled the windows.

We lay in my bed, lolling in the heat we created, watching the fire flicker and leap from the gas logs.

"You do dangerous things," he said. "I'm hearing more and more stuff you've done."

"Like what?"

"Punching Salt Eldritch in Custer's. You could have been banished from your favorite diner. Pretty risky."

I smiled. "Well, that backfired because Salt later tried to kill me."

"'Stupid, stupid, dead,' that's what Beulah said."

"Well, you can tell me you think something is dangerous, but if I decide to go through with it, don't you dare impede me."

"What would you do if I did?"

"Dump you."

"Man alive, that's harsh."

"Maybe so. But right now I have zero tolerance for any crap in my life."

"Fine, I'll remember that. So, um, I've kind of been talking around it—Christmas that is—but I was hoping you would come home with me."

"To meet the family. Have we been dating long enough for that? Christmas would only mark a couple of months for us."

"Two and a half. And I've met your family."

"Well, there are so few people out here, it would be hard not to."

"I'm staying here for Thanksgiving."

"And that's great, really. But, um, the idea of it, not your family per se, but just the thought of showing up in the midst of all those people and all that…uh…family merriment makes me sweat. But I promise to think on it."

"Fair enough."

The Percival funeral was held a week later on a Saturday. After the service at my Presbyterian church, I approached Kenny and Helen as they stood in the social hall in the church basement.

"You two are doing well," I said. "I usually go through funeral services in a trance which people mistake for bravery."

Kenny looked at me with a strange expression.

"We were at your dad's funeral," he said.

"Mr. Wilson's, too," said Helen.

I nodded. "I saw Celeste at the service, but I don't see her now."

"Oh, she went home to be with Mitch so the boys could come," said Helen.

A tall man with dark hair stood in line for the luncheon sandwiches just a few people ahead of Bill and Mom. Helen stared intently at the stranger.

"Is that Buster standing in line?" I asked.

"Dang, could be," said Kenny. "It's been years and he never liked me so he stayed away from us. Had a soft spot for Mitch. They got along pretty good."

Helen smiled. "Buster used to keep hard candy in his pocket. Mitch would go up to him and clap his hands and point to the pocket and Buster would give him one. I bet neither remembers that. Wonder where he's been all these years."

78   LIES IN THE WIND

"Hard to say. But you two better get in line before your sons eat up all the sandwiches."

I smiled at them then joined my Mom and Bill.

"Is that Buster up ahead?" asked Mom.

"I don't know, probably. Hey, um, try to get a photo or two of him. People watch me too closely. Just pretend that you're messing with your phone, like it's new and you're showing Bill. Beulah's behind you. She'll play along. Maybe she even remembers him."

"Aren't you staying?" Bill asked.

"No, I've had enough. Is Patty any better?"

"No, says she's got a wicked sore throat. She finally gave in and went to the doctor, so she's on an antibiotic."

"Well, I'll go home and send her texts. See ya."

Monday morning, I checked my appointments for the day and noted the addition of a name made just minutes ago—Darold Redmond. I went to the kitchen to get a cup of coffee and one of Glenda's Monday brownies. I considered my line of questioning for him, deciding to take a more laid-back position—I certainly didn't want to alert him to my participation in the investigation of the murders.

Promptly at eleven o'clock, Glenda showed him in to my office. Buster looked just as I thought he would—tall, with dark hair and forty or so. He must have inherited more of the Sioux genes than Val, for his skin was darker than hers, but not as dark as Patty's. He'd made an effort to look respectable; still, his navy twill pants and his blue and white checked shirt still displayed the fold creases, as if he got dressed just after purchasing the clothes from Clark's a few minutes ago. A handsome man, he looked to be in good health, though his smile revealed poor teeth, a sure indicator of someone living from one paycheck to the next in rural America.

Small talk revealed that he'd not heard of Val's death right away because he went from job to job in Cherry County, doing mostly handyman and carpentry work along with some fence repair. He'd found out about Val's death only a few days ago from a distant cousin.

Despite his friendly manner, he repulsed me. I don't know why, but my insides swirled and my bones wanted to dash to the door. I wanted him to go away, though his next comment roused my interest.

"I've heard you rent a nice duplex. Would like to stay in the area awhile. I been livin' from one motel to the next, in my car at times, eatin' fast food. Kinda like the idea of spendin' the winter someplace nice and warm. Got family nearby. I drove by the place...looks nice."

"Well, I do have the east side available for rent. You can rent by the month. Now the family next door has two small kids, so I'd expect you to keep the noise down and not bother them. And smoking is not allowed in the house or garage."

"Oh, I understand. I'd like me a garage for the winter. Saved enough money to get me by for a while."

I didn't like this man, but I did like rental payments, even if he only paid for a month then skipped out on me. And I wouldn't begrudge a man the opportunity to be around family at Christmas.

"Miss Beulah at the diner said it's furnished...has a kitchen."

"That's right." I liked the idea of keeping this man nearby, to see if anyone had seen him around—especially in Dexter at the time of the murders. "I can take you out there at noon. I do have a phone conference in a few minutes, but I think we can make you comfortable for a bit. Tell me, what's your opinion of homemade brownies?"

He smiled. "Oh, Lord. Haven't had me homemade anything forever."

I called for Melanie, who quickly appeared at the door.

"Mr. Redmond will be waiting in the lobby for a few minutes then I'm taking him out to the duplex. Will you make sure he gets a brownie or two and a cup of coffee?"

LIES IN THE WIND

"Certainly," said Melanie, who kept her gaze on me, for this was an unusual request of her.

"And Mr. Redmond—"

"Oh, shoot, call me Buster. And I thank you for your kindness, Miz Docket."

"Okay, Buster, I'll need your driver's license and three references. Melanie will collect those from you. You can leave a check for the first month's rent of $450.00 with her, too."

When I stood, he did, also.

"I'll see you at noon," I said.

He followed Melanie out the door. I immediately sent her a text that read: "potential murder suspect. Get photos of him and his car license. Make copy of dr lic and check."

Then I rang Jay, but had to leave a message. I called Merritt to tell him of Buster's arrival and that he'd be renting the east half of my duplex.

Why did he bother me? He didn't seem smart, though people can pull out the hayseed shtick to fool others. I didn't feel a sense of danger, but that didn't rule out a deceitful nature. Still, there was something.

At noon, he followed me out to the duplex in a 1990s green Chevy pickup with a matching topper. He could carry all his possessions in two large suitcases. I lagged behind to photograph his truck from the front and the rear. I didn't plan to ask, but he said he had been working in Cherry County, yet his truck bore expired South Dakota license plates. He expressed his pleasure with the two-bedroom duplex, stating he'd never lived in anyplace so big. Anxious to get away from him and to lunch, I was disappointed when he stopped me as I walked out to the Barracuda.

"Oh, just one more question, Miz Docket. I have this phone number for Kenny and Helen…I wanted to go visit them. I thought I might take Mitch a gift. Do you have any ideas?"

"In fact, I do. I gathered Mitch's DVDs from his house so I know of some good movies he doesn't have." I took out a notebook and wrote down three Pixar DVDs—*Wall-E*, *The Incredibles*, and *UP*. "These are good movies that even adults like, so the whole family will like them."

"Um, how much do they cost?" he asked.

"Oh, just buy one. I'll buy the others. I don't know if they have Blu-ray, so get the standard format." I handed him $60.00 from my billfold. "I actually owe Mitch one. When I bagged up his DVDs, I left Cinderella behind. This is a tough time for Helen and Kenny…they don't need to listen to singing mice and an evil stepsister singing off-key."

Buster was still laughing as I climbed into my SUV. At least he had a sense of humor.

At Custer's, I met Mom for lunch. Beulah shuffled up to our table.

"Heh, heard Patty's sick, that's too bad," she said. "Hey, I seen that Buster here earlier. Spent most of the mornin' here, eatin' and readin' the paper. He told me he had an appointment with you."

"He did. I'm renting half of the duplex to him. Did you talk about anything else?"

"Oh, this and that. I said I saw him at the funeral on Saturday."

"Well, chat him up, if you get the chance," I said.

Beulah squinted her eyes at me. "Hmm. Somethin' fishy?"

"I just wonder about him. Did you remember him from when he used to visit?"

"That's been awhile. No, I can't say I recall him…not exactly. I remembered he was tall and dark, but that's all. Didn't come here but a time or two."

"How long has he been gone, do you think?"

She rubbed her chin with her veiny hand. "Mmm, seven, eight years maybe, but it's hard to say. Natural for him to come back for the funeral."

"Oh, of course. He seems nice enough."

"Hmm," she said and wandered off.

Mom was staring hard at me.

I leaned forward and said, "As Val's brother, he stands to come into some life insurance money."

"I noticed Melanie was tending to him. She took his picture. Did you see the one I took at the funeral?"

"Yeah, it's pretty good. But that new paint in the basement of the church changes people's complexion."

"He looks like he's got some Sioux or something in him," she said.

"His father Howard was half Lakota. Oh, did you finish scanning all those files?"

"Yes. I finished the Percival files this morning."

"Good."

"Do you want me to start on some others?" she asked.

"Nah, you need to get out of the dungeon for a while."

The next evening, Celeste stopped by for a chat and a root beer float.

"What did you think of Buster?" I asked as we sat at the kitchen table.

"He was, like, clueless, stupid really. He didn't seem to recall much...knew our names and ages and where Mom and Dad worked...but he didn't remember much else. Maybe he's a drinker...I heard lots of drinking messes with your memory."

"Did he remember the candy in the pocket for Mitch?"

"Didn't seem to, but he didn't really go near Mitch. We liked the movies he bought us. So, he knows something."

"Maybe not. I gave him that list of movies to buy. But that doesn't matter. Did he mention he's staying awhile?"

"Yeah, said you're renting half of a duplex for him."

"So, are your folks okay with me or still mad?"

"Oh, good. They seem to think you're the one keeping my dad out of jail."

I nodded. That wasn't necessarily true, but I'd let them think that if it gave me their cooperation and trust.

"Hey, Noah and Ryan want to bring Mitch out to your hills, or whatever you call it, like you suggested."

"It's supposed to be a decent weekend and it's dry out there. What about Saturday afternoon? You should come with them."

"I'm off at two, we could come after that."

"Great." I scooped my last spoonful of ice cream then drank the rest of the creamy root beer. "Celeste, I think it's a shame you're not in college."

"I had the grades for it. I even took the ACT. But my dad thinks I'm stupid. Says he's not gonna waste money on me. It's like he sees me only as a pot head. I haven't done any of that since jail. I even stopped smoking."

"I noticed."

"My mom doesn't say much, it hurt her when I got busted, but it was only a misdemeanor. And she doesn't like my friends. I'm not sure I do either." She set her glass down on the table. "Dad says waitressing is good enough for me but then he talks about college for my brothers."

"You need to prove him wrong."

"How?"

"Go to college and do well."

"I hardly earn enough for that. And loans…dang, getting a load of debt scares me."

"You must not know about the Docket Law scholarship program. It's nothing official, but we're helping one of Bill's cowhands start at UNK in January."

"Oh, I'd like going to Kearney. Lots of my classmates went there."

"Why don't you collect the information on tuition, room and board, and fees then we'll see what we can do. Keep it to yourself, though. I can't help more than a couple of students."

"Yeah, great. I'll do that. Thanks."

"He likes texture," said Noah.

He, Celeste, Ryan, and I stood watching Mitch roll the lavender-gray buffalo grass in his fingers. Once and awhile, he'd put the grass to his lips to feel it then roll it back between his fingers. Then he walked over to the rocky mound to run his fingers along the rocks and dirt. Celeste walked over and picked up Mitch's gloves, abandoned to better explore the strange ground.

"That's Sleepy," I said. "Vonny Wilson named these the Seven Dwarfs."

"Where are you hiding the other two?" asked Ryan.

"Well, she couldn't count yet," I said. "Just where it flattens out to the east is where we caught the guys who set that cross on fire."

"The Four Bastards," said Noah. "And you were the ringleader, I heard. The Ghost Rider."

"They were bastards, scaring Mr. Wilson like they did," said Ryan. "I'm glad they got shot."

"Well, we caught them, so I retired. Sometime we can show Mitch the horses, see what he thinks of them."

We followed Mitch as he walked over the next small butte.

"What did you think of Buster?" I asked.

Ryan shrugged. "Don't really care. He's ignored us all these years. He can go back where he came from."

"Weird that he didn't, like, go near Mitch," said Noah. "They were buddies when Mitch was little."

I turned to hear the voices in the northwest wind. Rather than soothing, James and Beverly were agitated, eerie. They were warning me of danger. But whose?

"There's something about Buster. I don't trust him. I'll give all of you my card. I want you to call me whenever he goes to your house. Watch him closely. If you feel super alarmed, call the police."

Celeste turned to me and the guys stepped in front of me.

"Tell us," said Ryan. "We're old enough to know."

"I don't doubt that. You three would be the ones a dangerous person would underestimate. You see, Mitch is worth money now—from his family's assets and from life insurance. He may be in danger. But I could be wrong. And I don't know who the threat comes from. It may be from some hacker who tries to get into his bank account. I just don't know."

"Is it a lot of money?" asked Celeste.

"We won't know the full extent for a while. But yes, to many people it would be a fair amount of money. He doesn't have it yet, but that may not matter."

"Our aunt and uncle were murdered for the money, weren't they?" said Ryan.

"Probably, but we won't know until we find the murderer. That's why I went behind the scenes to get the State Patrol involved."

"Do they think my dad killed them?" asked Noah.

"There is circumstantial evidence that points to him and some that doesn't. They don't know who did it. I don't think it was your dad. So here's a question I want you to think about because you know the family. Who is smart?"

"Smart? Because they tried to frame my dad," said Celeste.

"Smart because they set it up to look like a murder-suicide then planted evidence against more than one person in case the police didn't believe it was a suicide."

"So, the State Patrol figured that out," said Ryan.

"No, I did. We better catch up to Mitch."

"How?" asked Celeste.

"I can't discuss that. But the murderer fooled the sheriff and deputies."

Celeste gave me a big smile. "So you called your boyfriend."

"Choose wisely whom you date. C'mon, Mitch is headed toward Pooper's Canyon."

I heard laughter behind me. I started running when Mitch did.

"Catch him, guys!"

Ryan and Noah passed me in a burst. The caught up to Mitch and turned back to me. I pointed north, so they steered him away from the edge. Ryan took a position between him and the ditch. Celeste and I caught up to them.

"We can walk along it so he can see it," I said of the gully. "It gets shallower as we go north."

We walked for a ways. Now and then Noah or Ryan would turn to look at me. We reached the edge of the gully. Mitch stared at the ground, probably wondering how it disappeared.

"Wanna see where I killed a man?"

"Yeah!" said Ryan, which was heartily affirmed by the other two.

By the time I narrated the night attack on James and me and the death of Salt Eldritch with the use of a steak knife, a rock, and the deep ditch dubbed Miss Gulch, it was time to take Mitch home for his afternoon snack.

As I handed them my business cards, I wrote my cell number on the back. Mitch looked closely at what they held, so I gave one to him, which seemed to please him. He immediately ran his fingers over the embossed blue ink. They all climbed in Celeste's rusty white Chevy.

They drove west onto Harney Street then north on Highway 51. I stood in my driveway as the frigid wind intensified, lashing at my body and stinging my face. God help me, I was going to do anything and everything to protect that boy and his family.

That meant finding a killer.

Chapter 10

WE left behind the altitude, the wind, and the bluffs then drove eastward through the flattest, dullest part of Nebraska. The interstate, like the historic Union Pacific railroad, cut across the smoothest route the land could provide. I'd spent time in the city of Grand Island, so I knew the only hill in town was an overpass. Some people didn't realize we possessed forested areas, and even canyons in Pine Ridge, something besides cornfields and cows. As we descended from the high plains, the flat land was marked by occasional groves of cottonwoods growing along the creeks and gullies, and conifers planted as wind blocks. The few inches of snow sparkled in the bright sunshine as we headed toward Omaha and its rolling hills.

I had consented to meet Jay's family over Christmas vacation. He was in high spirits; it amused me as I sipped my Earl Grey and drove the first half of the six-hour drive in the Barracuda. Jay said it would impress his family. I wondered if he meant the SUV or the fact that I named my vehicles after marine life.

"Did you know Alfred Hitchcock was afraid of eggs, policemen, and children?" he asked.

"That's weird…wait…he had at least one child because you said his daughter played the other secretary in Psycho."

"Yeah, well, maybe it was okay if the kid was his. And the stuff that looks like blood going down the drain in the shower scene is really chocolate syrup. "

"But you can't tell in black and white," I said.

"Right. He insisted the movie be filmed in black and white or it would be too graphic and never get by the censors. And the plot—he kills off the protagonist in the middle of the movie. Who does that?"

"Then Norman Bates becomes the focus. Yeah, that shift is bizarre, but it works."

He continued with more trivia as I sipped my tea. We stopped at a rest area to eat our lunch—sandwiches I brought in a cooler. I despised fast food—it made my stomach gurgle and otherwise complain. He let me sleep for next the hour as he drove. When I awoke, I told him about Mitch's excursion into my backyard.

"I asked Celeste, Ryan, and Noah who they thought was smart among their male relatives. Celeste says they talked about it, and decided Fred and Dave were smart enough to make it through college. And Fred was sneaky-smart. They didn't think Buster was dumb, but maybe not intelligent. Of the Redmonds, Gage is smart, Grant is a dud, and Greg is smart but in North Platte, though he came for the funeral. Oh, and the kids don't think their dad did the murders and they don't put him in the smart category either."

"Interesting," said Jay. "That pretty much agrees with the assessments of Merritt and Rachel, though she said both Gage and Grant hit on her."

"They're lucky she kept her cool. Anyway, what do we have for alibis for those guys?"

"Buster has been evasive, says he's been working here and there or something equally vague, but we confirmed his location with a rancher in Cherry County on the day of the murders. Fred says he was driving out to a client, who wasn't at home so he drove back to Kimball. So no alibi there. Dave was in his office, as confirmed by his staff. And Gage left the Percival house before lunch and his brother says he returned to Werner Electric for the rest of the day and never left."

"So, Buster, the one most likely to benefit, is the only one with an apparently independent witness as to his whereabouts," I said. "And money is still the only motive we have for the murders."

"I agree. Oh, and we figured out why it was so hard to track Buster—he'd been in a Canadian prison for four years on an assault and battery charge."

"Well, I'll get a chance to judge the Redmond brothers. I've hired Werner Electric in Kimball to complete the wiring in the new conference room. Both Gage and Grant will be working at the firm."

"If one of them is the killer, that's dangerous."

"The staff will be on alert. Those guys will never be left on the premises alone and they won't be getting keys to the building. They start January second. They'll never know it's anything more than a job."

He was quiet for a few minutes. I waited for him to argue against my involvement with the Redmond brothers; instead, he surprised me.

"Just a warning…well, two. My family really liked Alison. They were disappointed when I broke it off."

"When did you date her?"

"We dated for three years. I even proposed. I called it off two years ago."

I was curious, so I let my silence give him a chance to talk about her if he wanted. Finally, I asked, "What's the other warning?"

"My sisters are annoyed I moved from Omaha. They think I'm caught up in hero worship."

"Huh?"

"You."

"Me?"

"Well, the news has been full of your adventures or 'incidents' as you call them. People call you the Annie Oakley of the Wild West."

"I killed the last person who called me Annie Oakley, but that's just a coincidence."

He laughed. "You don't talk to the press, but you're still famous out here."

"Yeah, but your sisters don't like me, even though they've never met me. What about your folks?"

"Oh, they're not so quick to criticize. They're much smarter."

My hands felt clammy and my nervousness made me quiet.

"What? C'mon, they'll love you."

I stayed silent, apprehension turned to dread.

"I shouldn't have told you."

I remained silent for a while and he didn't press me. After twenty minutes or so, I said, "Maybe this was a mistake."

"No, Megan. It'll be fine."

"Maybe I should go stay with one of my aunts."

"No, babe. No. My sisters aren't clods, they'd never say anything mean."

I was now in a panic. How was I to solve this? I was not ready.

"Let's pull off," I said.

"What? I didn't think it would upset you so much."

"Oh, because I'm so tough, so hard...I get it...because I've killed people. But this is family stuff. I think it's more frightening. Maybe another time is better."

"C'mon. I've seen you chew up and spit out bigger, tougher people...and that's just in court."

"You don't understand, maybe you can't. This is the messy stuff of families and you don't know about lies and discord and separation and death. Your parents are alive and your siblings are alive. Your sisters even have kids—I have a daughter, a brother, and a father deep in the frozen ground. Here's a rest stop. Please pull off."

"Oh, babe. Okay."

As soon as he pulled into a parking spot, I bolted from the SUV, sucking in the cold fresh air. I felt my tears freeze onto my cheeks. He can't understand. I felt trapped. It wouldn't look good if I backed out now. But it made me want to vomit. He walked up beside me.

"And I don't like the idea of staying with your parents…in your old room. We aren't married and I'm recently divorced."

"I didn't realize you were still so wounded by all of this," he said.

I wanted to bolt, but there weren't any bluffs, just grain silos in the distance and they wouldn't do.

"Megan, please talk to me."

"Right now, I'd rather go back to jail."

"You didn't just say that."

I jerked forward and knelt down, choked by dry heaves. Then I looked up at the sky. Peace, I just can't find it. Instead, I consented to entrapment. Jay came and lifted me to my feet.

"How 'bout this…we'll get a hotel room. Then you have some place quiet to be alone when you need to be. Too bad I've sublet my condo. If you go to your aunt's, you just have to deal with that part of your family history. And there would be questions. Please, give me and my family a chance. They won't disappoint you."

An hour later, we registered in a west Omaha Marriott. While I unpacked, Jay stood near the window talking on his cell phone, stumbling through an excuse as to why we'd decided to stay in a hotel. After he said goodbye, he stood next to me with a look I'd never seen before; perhaps he finally saw me as I was—wounded. I wanted my clients and most everyone else to think I was strong, but those close to me needed to understand that my losses, my ordeals cut me deeply. Then he did the smartest thing he could do—he hugged me, not in a sexual way, for usually our embraces ended with love making—this was pure comfort. It was love and kindness without the need for any words.

"When do they expect us?" I said.

He smiled and kissed me. "Anytime you're ready."

I let Jay drive to his parents' house, a beige tri-level in west Omaha. The moment I stepped out of my SUV, everything seemed out of kilter. The parents, Jerry and Sue, greeted us at the door. They were polite, though Sue acted fluttered. The eldest sister, Amy, was friendly, as was Trish. Yet it smacked of stiffness. Somebody needed to tell a joke or crack a genuine smile.

Jerry said the grandkids were all playing Barbies or G.I. Joes in the basement. I wanted to join them, for they couldn't be any more rigid than this bunch. Trish, a divorcée, was soon joined by her boyfriend, Jon.

As he took off his coat, he looked at me and said, "So this is the great warrior. You're dinky for an Amazon."

Trish laughed like she'd never heard anything funnier in her life. In time, we could probably work through coldness, but I wondered how I could hold my tongue in the midst of two obnoxious people. I wanted to play Barbies, no, I wanted my keys from Jay so I could bolt in my SUV.

Amy grabbed my arm and pulled me away.

"Don't bother with her. She's always had a cockle bur up her butt."

That was funny, but I wasn't ready to laugh. I did manage to smile.

The roast beef dinner was very good, but I found it hard to eat. Trish asked me a question, but I ignored her—she wasn't worth my time. Jerry and Sue tried to warm things up and Amy attempted friendliness. Her husband, Eric, was cordial; he even asked me about a recent Supreme Court decision. Okay, things were getting better. Jay jumped in with a do you remember story that got us all laughing.

Jay was drinking a glass of milk with his supper, so I asked, "Are you going to drink a whole gallon this evening?"

Even Trish laughed over Jay's youthful dairy feat. Amy told of the time Jay licked one side of all the Pringles in a can so he could eat them all. We all laughed again. Maybe I was going to be okay with this group. After supper in the family room, Sue and Amy served root beer floats. Jay gave me a wink. He was trying so hard. The conversation turned to Nebraska football.

"Some people still say that ninety-six Husker team was one of the greatest ever," said Jerry.

"Dad, that was the ninety-five team," Jay said softly.

"Oh, er, right."

After a few minutes of discussion of the weather, Jerry asked, "How is your practice going?"

"It's very busy," I said. "In fact, I recently hired another attorney for my firm."

"Oh, ah, lots of criminals out there?"

"I don't do any criminal practice."

"Oh, er, right."

The poor man looked mortified at another gaffe.

"But the new attorney does some criminal work," I said, trying to assuage him.

He looked down at his empty glass. I felt sorry for him. He knew he wasn't coming off well. Later, Jay and I took our empty glasses into the kitchen. Sue was loading the dishwasher. Amy took our glasses from us.

"I'm sorry…ah…I heard you lost your baby," said Sue. "I'm sorry. You must miss him."

"Mom, it was a girl," said Jay, who looked annoyed.

"Yes, right, a girl," she said.

"Thank you," I said, but she had already turned away in embarrassment.

I was among idiots and obnoxious people, but I resolved to keep trying, at least for Jay, who was rubbing his temples. I preferred to stay in the kitchen, but Amy led Jay and me back into the family room. Trish was standing in the foyer talking on her phone. She ended her conversation quickly when she saw we'd returned.

"Hey, I think we should go to Arthur's," she said.

It was a west Omaha bar. This was strange; I was supposed to be getting to know the family.

"Oh, c'mon, it'll be fun."

"Fine with me," said Jon.

Eric shrugged, but Amy put her hands on her hips as she stood in the doorway.

"Mom and Dad can watch the kids," said Trish. "We won't stay long."

Amy gave in then Jay did. Soon I was in my coat and back in the Barracuda, feeling my guts churn. What next?

The bar was appropriately crowded for a Friday night. Christmas was still two days away, so it didn't yet have the dismal feel of the lonely seeking solace in strangers. Trish ordered a pitcher of light beer, which I considered pathetic. Why bother with beer if you weren't going to drink the real stuff? But I resolved to be a good sport. Just as I was beginning to relax and enjoy the live rock band, a tall woman with blonde streaks in her hair walked up to our table. Jay quickly identified her as an old girlfriend, the last one he dated before he started his undercover work in the panhandle. She was attractive, about twenty-five and wore skinny jeans and a glitter top. I said hello then turned to talk to Amy. Christine talked so loud I wondered if she was already drunk. When she grabbed onto Jay's arm, I just shook my head as she laughed. When Christine dropped her drink on the floor, both she and Trish laughed. It appeared the two women were friends. Christine continued to hang onto to Jay's arm, but spoke to Trish.

Amy and Eric got up and left soon afterwards. The band took a break and Jay went to the restroom. Christine was staring at me, so I turned away. Jon was watching an NHL game on a TV over the bar. I watched the game for a few minutes. Jay talked to a man with a crew cut who looked like a cop. I turned back to the game.

"This looks good for Pittsburgh," I said to Jon who sat nearby on a high barstool, the kind I hated because my feet dangled in the air. "They've got the lead and Crosby fresh off the bench."

Jon smiled at me and we began discussing hockey. He looked back at Trish and Christine.

"Sorry about the Amazon remark," he said.

"That's all right. Don't you think it's interesting that an old girlfriend just happens to show up here? Did Trish call her?"

"I don't know. She can be that way."

Jay returned to the table. A few moments later, Christine groaned.

"Oh, my God, I'm feeling dizzy. I gotta go."

"You can't drive," said Trish. "But I think Jon and I will go. C'mon, Jon."

He shrugged and helped Trish on with her coat. In a flash they were gone. Shit. We'd need to take care of the bimbo.

"We should call her a cab," I said.

"No! My car. It's new—I can't leave it here overnight."

I glowered at the vixen.

"All right, I'll drive your car to your apartment and Megan can follow in her car," said Jay.

I stared at him. This was a bad idea, said my bones. Then I sensed it coming—I jumped off my stool and to the side just as Christine leaned forward on the table and knocked over Trish's glass of beer onto the table and the stool where I'd been sitting.

"Oops!" she said laughing, though she failed to get me.

"Let's go," said Jay, who grabbed Christine's arm and yanked her toward the door.

I followed as I put on my coat. I didn't like this at all, but at least we'd be rid of her. I pulled the Barracuda behind the Honda Civic Jay was loading Christine into. It wasn't a late model car and it didn't have dealer plates. Jay walked around to the driver side and looked back at me. He'd know I was pissed. I followed them a few miles to an apartment complex. They both seemed to wobble as they made their way to the door. Yeah, goodbye, you lying bitch.

I sat in the warmth of the Barracuda. Five minutes. Good grief, did he have to carry her up the stairs? Had she lost her keys? Ten minutes. I turned off the ignition. This was getting beyond pathetic. Fifteen minutes. Pathetic was now transforming into anger. What the hell? Was he listening to some sob story? Would she try to seduce him? Surely, he wouldn't be so stupid to risk a romp with her while I sat waiting for him outside the building. Despite my burning indignation, I was getting cold. Thirty minutes. What a son of a bitch. I drove back to the hotel. I found a dinky bottle of Jack Daniels in the mini bar. I drank a glass then another, despite my churning guts. I paced the room. My awful day ended in a nightmare. I chained the door and set the deadbolt. Was he trying to make me jealous? Test me? Play games? This was risky considering my reluctance to even come for the visit.

I lay in bed, wide awake. All that had passed between us was erased—he'd screwed it away. And I'd believed the things he told me—what an idiot I was. How could he do something so blatant and not understand the consequences? If he meant to make me feel like a fool, he'd succeeded.

In time, the bourbon floated me to sleep. But I awoke before dawn, angry and resolved. Buddy, we're done. I packed my things, downed a couple of Advil, and dropped my key-card on the bed. On the way out of town, I was forced to eat a fast food breakfast, which turned my sour stomach rancid. A large coffee kept me alert and furious. Daylight came and I chomped on several Rolaids. What a son of a bitch!

This man I thought was wonderful turned out to be another screw-up in my list of lovers. I guess I really didn't know him. And his family—oh, brother! His parents were bumbling idiots, his oldest sister was clueless, and that bitch Trish was a schemer. Good riddance to them all.

My phone rang, it was Jay. I ignored it. At a rest stop, I read his text asking me where I was. "Getting far away from you," I texted back.

He texted me again, saying he needed to explain last night to me.

I responded, "Stay away from me. We are done."

LIES IN THE WIND

I ignored the subsequent calls and texts. Yet the tears came. I'd be steadfast in rejecting him, but it hurt so badly. I pulled off near Cozad so I could sob without being a danger to other drivers. I thought I'd found someone special, someone who, in time, could come to understand me, despite my oddness, and truly love me. This was a rotten time for me to realize I loved him.

Chapter 11

I unpacked, ate lunch, and then trudged down the block. I needed my mommy. She and Bill listened to my narrative, stunned.

"I keep thinking I know these men—Brian, Zane, now Jay—but I guess I really don't," said my uncle.

"Brian fell in love with the new attorney, daddy's little puppet...but he couldn't deal with me after I'd passed through the ordeals of losing Dad and Scott, and became the boss of the firm...and maybe I changed in other ways. But with Jay, he was learning about me and starting to understand me as I was. But he's just another disappointment, another screw-up."

Mom sat down next to me on the sofa and wrapped her arms around my shoulders.

"I'm so sorry, hon," she said. "I know you're hurting."

"So, will you come have Christmas with us?" asked Uncle Bill. "I haven't missed a Christmas with you since you were a tot. I didn't like thinking I would."

"Yeah, I'll be here in the morning. But you two need to go on with your plans to go to Omaha on Monday. I'll stay here, so make my excuses, but go see your family, Mom."

She nodded, but sadness was imprinted on her face.

Later in the afternoon, I walked home from Bill and Mom's. Derek was coming back from the mailbox. He walked over.

"Hey, you're supposed to be in Omaha. What's up?" he asked.

"I'll just say Jay did me wrong and we're done."

"Well, dang. We're here if you need us. We leave in the morning after church for Denver."

"Okay, have fun."

Just as I turned to close the front door, Jay's truck pulled into my driveway. I really wasn't interested in whatever he had to say. But as soon as Jay walked up the sidewalk, Derek came to meet him.

"What did you do to her?" Derek shouted in Jay's face.

"I made a mistake," Jay replied.

"You hurt her."

Derek nailed Jay in the jaw knocking him to the ground. Jay stayed down, looking woozy.

Tina came sprinting coatless into my yard. "Derek! Stop! God above, you just hit a white cop!"

Jay rose to his knees. "No, it's just me."

"Derek, thanks, but stop," I said enjoying the sight of that bastard still trying to get to his feet. "Jay, just get lost."

Derek and Tina backed away.

"Aren't you even going to listen to what I have to say?" Jay asked.

"No, I don't think I care."

As I started to close the door, he lunged across the porch and caught the door in his left hand, the edge of the threshold in his right. He was so stupid to expose himself that way, and he paid for it. My kick to his balls dropped him to his knees and then to his back. Derek and Tina paused to catch the scene then went home.

"What exactly did you tell your parents and sisters about me? It's like they expected me to show up with six shooters at my hips." I asked as he sucked in air. "Your parents were blithering idiots, Amy was clueless and spineless as to the conniving tactics of Trish, and Trish is a bossy bitch, who set us up for Christine to destroy. And you were too stupid to see any of it. Who takes their girlfriend home to meet the parents then goes to a bar?"

Jay rolled onto his hands and knees. "I didn't want to go."

"Then why didn't you say something? I would have backed you. We should've stayed with your folks and played cards or something. Do you always let that sneaky bitch tell you what to do? What a pathetic wuss. You said they wouldn't disappoint me. Well, you and your family make me want to puke."

This time I did close the door. I locked the door and even rammed the floor bolt into its slot then went to the other doors and did the same. I closed the curtains on the main level. I'd hurt him physically—it seemed an appropriate act for someone who had screwed his way out of a relationship with me. I'd nailed Brian, too, when I caught him coming out of the shower with an Italian whore. Why do people think they can mess with me?

I spent the next day with Mom, Bill, and Patty. We did our best to have a nice day. That evening, while Mom and Bill finished packing, Patty and I watched White Christmas with Bing Crosby and Rosemary Clooney. An incredibly sappy movie, it was just what I needed. When Danny Kaye and Vera-Ellen danced to "The Best Things Happen When You're Dancing," I was completely transported from my troubles for three solid minutes.

After Patty left, I went up to my room and played my Luciano Pavarotti Christmas album, crying though all eleven songs—it had been my dad's favorite. Then I took from my dresser drawer a snapshot of Scott, my twin, then cried over the loss of him. I went to bed emotionally exhausted and dehydrated.

In the meantime, I continued to ignore Jay's calls and texts. On Monday, I spent the entire day reading the Percival, Goblet, and Redmond files on my secure laptop. I noted a few points of interest; otherwise, I didn't find much to shed light on the murders or the probable suspects. Could I be looking at this all wrong? Was it really about money? What about the famous feud that was nothing more than words and an occasional barroom fistfight? Was there more to it? And was this enough money for anybody to commit two murders? Except for Buster, nobody even possessed a criminal record—a few speeding tickets among the three families was the extent of the law-breaking. If not money, then what was the motive for the killings?

On the face of it, nobody committed two murders. So that was the next step—to delve under the surface.

On Tuesday, I went into the office to work. It was closed for the holiday, so it was nice and quiet. At eleven-thirty, I went out to the Barracuda, to drive home for lunch. On the driver side of the Barracuda was Jay, who stood up-right from a crouch. He must have tracked my SUV then waited for me to leave for lunch.

"Won't you give me two minutes to explain? Please," he said.

"You'll either try to convince me of some excuse or you'll beg forgiveness. I'm not interested in either. You're a pathetic pile of shit."

"Please, just let me tell you—"

"On our first real test as a couple you fail me in the most foul way. The sight of you makes me sick."

He winced, but blurted out, "She drugged me. At the bar…probably when I went to the restroom."

I confess I hadn't expected this excuse.

"I awoke on the floor of her apartment at four in the morning with a wicked headache. I knew I would need to explain it all to you, so I took a taxi to the ER to get a blood test. Dad came and got me from there. I left for here as soon as my head cleared. I have the hospital discharge record."

He took a yellow page from his inside coat pocket and held it out to me. I didn't move.

"Mom and Dad were so pissed when Trish admitted she saw Christine put something in my drink. Trish says it was only supposed to make me act goofy. Dad got mad then kicked Trish and her kids out of the house on Christmas Day. They aren't talking to her. She keeps calling me and leaving messages saying she's sorry, but I plan to ignore her."

"Did you screw her?" I asked.

"I-I can't see how...ah...I don't know."

"You and your family are so pitiful."

"But I was drugged."

"There's a difference between chivalry and stupidity. You obviously don't know it. I suggested a taxi, but you ignored me. Now get out of my way."

He did back up as I swung the door open. That kick to the balls wouldn't be forgotten and would make him keep his distance. I backed up then drove out of the parking lot toward home.

So he was drugged. It didn't make him seem less pathetic. And what a family—he'd made them sound so wonderful with his endearing childhood tales. He never mentioned Trish was a deceitful viper. He'd made sure he painted them in the best light. What else didn't I know? He may have cheated on me or maybe he didn't. I might never know. He was a chump either way. Nobody should be forced to deal with this crap. And he'd opened yet another wound—once I got him out of my life, it would close.

Back in my office after lunch, I called Robert Foxworthy, my FBI contact in Denver. He knew about the double homicide in Dexter then added that he was certain I'd be involved. I asked if he knew anything about illegal activities for any of the potential suspects in the Goblet, Redmond, or Percival families. He promised to check and get back to me.

Next I called Al Carlsson at State Farm to advise that suicide was ruled out by the State Patrol. Then I said this conversation must be kept in confidence. I told him that I would withhold my report recommending life insurance be disbursed because one of the beneficiaries was still a suspect in the double murders and that a conservatorship had not been completed, for one of the conservators was also a murder suspect. He said he'd communicate my unofficial opinion to the life insurance company. I stressed that he should do so verbally to avoid leaving any evidence for disgruntled beneficiaries to find.

I then left a message for my contact at Aztec Mutual. The return call came from a company vice president. I told her of my concerns regarding potential beneficiaries and potential murder suspects. She agreed to keep the information off the record and to withhold funds. She then told me the Goblet insurance agency was under investigation for selling fraudulent life insurance and long term health care policies. I thanked her for the information then promptly reported the information to Foxworthy.

That night I climbed into bed, shivered, got up then put on jammie pants and socks. Tomorrow I'd go buy the electric blanket I'd seen at Ritter's hardware. Paul knew he couldn't compete with Sidney's Wal-Mart or mail order, so his store became a hodge-podge of goods—things for people who didn't want to wait for the mail or drive into Sidney or Kimball or who just tried to support the local shops. So tomorrow I'd get that blanket. It wasn't as if Jay was here every night to warm me, but tonight I felt especially cold.

Lord above, how I hurt. Dammit, I loved that man, but why put up with the pain? I lit the fireplace and climbed once more back into bed. His touch, his voice, his smell, his kindness—it all haunted me. Why did I give in? We'd still be dating if I had been honest and refused to go see his family. It was too early in our relationship for such an act. He hadn't experienced much loss or pain in his life, so he was less cautious, less understanding. Yet, I missed him so badly—how was I to sleep when my innards were twisted and my heart was shredded?

Yet morning came at last. I went down to the basement to run on the treadmill and watch the morning news. At the firm, nobody knew my pain, for Mom wasn't there; she would be driving back from Omaha today with Bill. I missed her reassuring smile. At ten, Beulah called and said she wanted to talk, but couldn't get away because the diner was so busy. I agreed to come for a late lunch then we could talk afterward. She'd be a welcome distraction.

Custer's was clearing out when I arrived at one o'clock. Two booths away sat Eldon Strumple and Melvin Poots, both retired ministers. I gave them a smile and a wave. Carol took my order then Beulah came and sat down across from me. EJ, Pastor Strumple's son and the cook at Custer's, came out and sat with the men.

"I want a living will," said Beulah. "A new one."

"Well, okay," I said, puzzled. "How do you want it to be different?" I took a notebook from my purse.

"I want you to be the agent...make sure it all goes right," she said.

"Well, I'm sure your nephews would do right by you."

"I talked to 'em. Told 'em I meant no offense. You see, Best Friend, if you could sit and watch James die...a man you loved like a father...then you would take care of me."

"Are you trying to make me cry?" I said with a grin and a lump in my throat.

"Oh, pshaw."

"I confess, I've been drafting quite a few living wills lately. Everybody should have one. Doctors love them. In fact, I should offer them for free."

"I'll take one," said Pastor Poots. "But I'll pay for it."

"Hello, Pastor Poots," I said.

Beulah scooted down the booth and said, "Have a seat, Mel."

Soon, I had moved down to make room for Pastor Strumple.

"Megan, call me Mel. I do have two daughters who would take care of me. But I should've gotten one of those wills long ago. Your father wrote the wills for my wife and me."

"How is Mrs. Poots?" I asked.

"Still in the nursing home, but it's not too far from the house. The home provided a living will for Pamela, so she's set. Heart's still bad."

"And she has rheumatoid arthritis, too, if I remember correctly."

"You do. I'm impressed."

I smiled at him. He was a short, wiry man with sparse dark gray hair, who appeared spry for his seventy-some years. The retired pastor at a church in Sidney, he lived on a two-acre spread once owned by his cousins.

"Do you still breed beagles?" I asked.

"Oh, my Charlotte had a litter this fall, but I think that'll be it for me. It can be a lot of work when they're young."

"I may have a buyer for you. My neighbors, Derek and Tina Wilson, have a dog, who's in serious need of grief counseling. That's hard to do with dogs, so my mom suggested the distraction of a puppy for him."

"Heh, that's what your son did for you, Eldon, got you that bulldog after Elaine died," said Beulah.

"Yeah, Charlie...he was a puppy and ton of trouble. Just what I needed."

"That's right...the dog," I said. "Eldon, you live next to the Percivals."

"Right," he said. "But I was at your office with you when the murders were committed. I recall that young woman, the niece, came and got you."

"Was Charlie outside at that time?"

"No, he was inside...he has that short hair, so I don't leave him out long. Those bulldogs got a cranky face, but Charlie is good-natured. Hank and Lew come out to visit him sometimes."

"Did the electricians working there ever come to see Charlie?"

"Ah, you're playing sleuth now. Yes, both Gage and Grant Redmond used to go over to see him. Charlie would've barked like crazy if a stranger had been around.

But he was friendly to Junior and Val and eventually Mitch...though he was too scared for a long time before he'd pet Charlie."

"Next to my Davey, that Mitch is the purest soul that ever lived," said Beulah. "You need brains to be deceitful. I admire that boy sometimes...misses out on so much of the trouble and pain the rest of us stir up."

We were quiet for a bit then Mel looked at me.

"You're wondering about Gage and Grant. We're all wondering who killed the Percivals. Grant was always the brawn, probably still is. Gage is the sly one, though I don't know that he was ever dangerous. Can't see him killing Val, his own kin. But he could have a temper. Lucille, Granny Goblet, as she's mostly known, did her best with those boys."

"I heard Lucy divorced Howard because he was mean," I said, trying to stir up some history.

"That's too kind for Howard," said Mel. "He drank and he beat Lucy. She had to get out to save her life. Then she tried to get the boys. Every time she went back for them, Howard would bring all four boys out and whip them, right in front of her. She went to your dad, Megan, but that just increased the abuse. She finally gave up...did what she could to help them behind Howard's back, but he turned those boys against her. No wonder she married again and tried to start anew. Howard tried to turn them against the Goblet kids, too. Lucy mostly kept them separate because the Redmonds were older and bigger."

"Heh! That's how Shiny got his name," said Beulah. "He got a black eye from Grant and that's when they were young men. They were playin' poker, and Gage accused Fred of cheating...which he probably was. So Grant pounded him. And the name stuck, 'specially since Fred hated it."

"How is Mitch?" asked Eldon.

"Adjusting slowly, from what Celeste Percival says, but getting better," I said. "People can only help from a distance, because he's so shy. She says sometimes he just sits and stares at the front door like he's waiting for his mom and dad to come for him."

Beulah ran her veiny hand across her face, never one to willingly let her emotions show.

Mitch also watched the Sidney and State Patrol cars that frequented the street in front of Kenny and Helen's house like it was entertainment for him. Word had gotten out that Mitch was in possible danger because of his position as a beneficiary. I didn't say anything else because I didn't want any questions about the life insurance. That was a fight looming in the near future.

Chapter 12

THE firm began the free living wills campaign in earnest, with Mom and Joy, my other assistant, sending out letters to existing clients. Kayla, Emily, and Chelsea, my young friends, sealed the envelopes and attached the stamps—obviously the girls were bored over their winter break. Beulah let me post a small placard at Custer's and Paul Ritter let me post one at his store. And Glenda, baker extraordinaire, doubled her production of pastries.

The day after we posted the signs, people started to come in; sometimes they even bothered to make an appointment. Gus, Rich, or I would explain the simple, one page document that essentially stated no extraordinary measures would be taken to keep them alive. I always showed my clients the language or read it to them. They liked the part that allowed for them to be kept comfortable. Then Joy, Mom, or Melanie would witness the drafted form, two were needed in Nebraska, and either send folks on their way or send them to Glenda for coffee and something sugary. Brian even witnessed some of the wills, hoping people would remember him at tax time.

As I hoped, Pearl Redmond, Val and Buster's mother, and Granny Goblet both made appointments for living wills. My dad drafted wills for them years ago; still, I made sure the extra time was allotted for their appointments to allow for family talk.

Meanwhile, Jay continued to call and I continued to ignore him then cry into my pillow at night. I wanted peace—dating destroyed it. One time I broke down and answered the phone.

"My family wants to apologize," he said.

"I'm not interested in giving any of them two seconds of my time. And it should be your apology. Ever since we met, you've pushed me, time and time again, no, smothered me—that's what you've done. Well, I need some air."

"I'm sorry. And if it makes you feel better, I'm no longer talking to Trish. Oh, and the Douglas County State Patrol has nabbed Christine twice for speeding. I still have friends there."

"That's nice," I said.

"Megan, I've apologized and explained what happened. But now I realize just how weak your feelings were for me."

"Once again, you're wrong. You crushed me. And I'm not willing to get hurt like that again. I'm done with pain, so I'm done with you. Bye."

After he thought that over for a few minutes, he called back, but I didn't answer.

The first appointment the next morning was with Smokey Lurch, the owner of Smokey's sales yard. I went out to greet him as Glenda handed him a cup of coffee and a cinnamon scone. He hobbled into the office with his bad left hip and his gray combed-over hair.

"So how are you, Smokey?"

"Oh, fine, fine," he said in his gruff, raspy voice.

"Hey, no nicotine gum. Did you break the habit?"

"Nah, still tryin'. Got those patches now."

"It's good you're still fighting," I said.

"Yep…ah, so, I'd like one of those living wills, though I insist on payin' for it."

"That's fine."

"But I wanted to ask, um, do I need a new will? I mean, now that my wife is gone. Your dad wrote it up years ago."

I searched through my records. "Here we are." I studied his will on my computer screen. "No, it looks fine, unless you want to change it. All of your assets went to your wife, so with Louise gone, everything goes to Milt, John, and Stacy equally."

"Good, good."

"Now, before we talk about the living will, I would like to ask you a question."

"Shoot."

"I heard from two different sources that Junior and Fred Goblet had been bickering. Did you ever see them arguing?"

"Yeah, I did. Mmm, a week or so before the murder. Fred came out to confront Junior. They were really mad, I could tell. Junior was wavin' some papers around. Then Fred hit Junior, but then Junior punched Fred, knocked him down. Milt was with me when we saw them. But Fred didn't have anything gettin' repaired on the lot. He never bought anything from us."

"Do you know what they were arguing about?"

"No, I didn't hear anything, but see, Milt and I were in the office lookin' out at them in the yard. After about ten minutes...maybe less...Fred just left and Junior went back to work. It didn't seem to be my business, so I let it be."

I nodded. "It's all so sad."

"Oh, it just broke me up...Junior and Val...dead. Didn't seem possible. Knew them for years. And they got that boy, Mitch. Junior was a good worker. The police came out here, and I told them all that I could, but I suppose I wasn't helpful. I just hope they find who did it."

"Me, too. By the way, did the police search Junior's work area?"

"Yeah, I took them into the shop. Junior never kept anything of value back there...didn't have a desk or nothin' like that, brought his lunch ever'day. Did have a family photo, but I mailed that to Kenny."

I spent the next few evenings at home or at Mom and Bill's with Patty. On New Year's Eve, Bill invited Hank, Lew, and Linda Eldritch over. Mom made nachos as a snack and we played poker; well, I sat it out with Patty and Linda as the others played.

"Hey, I heard Buster Redmond is in town and renting from you, Megan," said Patty.

"Here, I have a photo of him on my phone, but it didn't turn out well," said Mom, "That new paint makes everybody look green and one of those fluorescent lights was flashing a bit."

Patty studied it. "It's been a long time. He'd be tall and this guy looks tall, but it's hard to tell from the face."

"I have better ones at work, but you'll probably see him sometime at Custer's," I said.

"The Redmond family is what got me out here from Fremont," said Patty. "Well, Shelly Metcalf did. She was a Redmond, a cousin to the family out here. But she died of breast cancer years ago. She thought most of the men in the family were drunks or thugs or both."

"The police had trouble tracking Buster because he'd spent a few years in a Canadian prison. He's been going job to job till someone tracked him down and told him about Val."

"It doesn't surprise me that he'd been locked up. The Redmonds are a violent bunch. Howard was the worst of them till Gary got big enough to give it back to him. Then the whippings stopped. Gary, as the oldest, got the most of it. Greg was the youngest, so he got less, but any was too much. Those boys never got a break—the beatings and then Lucy running away to save her skin."

"I heard she tried to get them back," I said.

"Yeah, Howard stopped that. It wasn't till after Howard died that they knew she tried to get them. Greg said the boys always felt abandoned. Then Gary died in Vietnam. That changed all of them...made 'em mean. I understood why Greg hit me—it was what he knew. But that didn't mean I had to take it. Once was enough."

I nodded. "So tell us about Gage and Grant."

"Well, mostly they're known to be good workers. Grant is dim-witted and Gage is smart and ambitious. Greg said Gage has always wanted to buy out old man Werner. If he ever gets the money, maybe he will. But the one thing all the Redmond men have in common is violence. Even the cousins, not just Howard's sons. They're a mean, nasty bunch. I was glad to be done with them." She ate a few bites of her nachos.

"But Howard's boys have always been around here, right?" I asked.

"Howard met Lucy in Alliance, but after that, yeah. All four of the boys worked at the supermarket in Sidney as sackers. Gage even worked his way up to delivering groceries to seniors. Then Grant and Greg followed Gage's lead and went to get vocational training as electricians."

"What about this feud I've heard about?" asked Mom.

"Oh, it was always just name-calling and drunken fights. The Redmond boys didn't bother Abby and Gabby, but they pounded on Fred and Dave, at least till Dave got bigger, well, never as tall as the Redmonds, but he was a wrestler in school and he picked up some boxing. Soon, Dave was whipping on Gage and Greg, when he could catch them alone. It seemed to fizzle out after high school, well, mostly."

"What do you know about Buster?" I asked.

"I didn't meet him till after Greg and I married. He was okay. He got into his share of trouble, Greg said, but none of it was around here. Assault and stealing cars, I think. Buster and Val grew up in Alliance, so he never got into the squabble with the Goblet family."

"Does it surprise you that he did time in a Canadian prison?" I asked.

"Not really, but I kinda thought he'd be settling down. He was smart enough for college, but just too wild, couldn't unwind, like he was ADD or something."

Great, another intelligent guy, but with an alibi—I wondered how strong it was. I sent Rachel a text when the game broke up. She answered immediately, which surprised me as I thought she'd be partying with her boyfriend. I accepted her proposal to meet tomorrow.

When I awoke the next morning, my guts were already starting to rumble. By half time during the first bowl game of the day, my guts were beginning to churn. I left Bill and Big Joe McCready in Bill's family room and found Mom and Patty in the kitchen. My mom's anxious stare bored another hole into the side of my head. I promised to call her later. I didn't want to involve them—I knew danger loomed ahead.

At home, I binged on chocolate then Rolaids. A half hour later, Rachel arrived.

"What's up with you?" Rachel asked. "You're acting strange and I've seen no evidence of Jay."

"I've stepped back," I said.

"Oh? So that's why he's been so cranky."

"I don't think I should talk too much about your boss. I'll just say I needed some air."

"And he was smothering you," she said. "Why do guys need to be so pushy? It's like they feel driven to prove they're not commitment phobic. Sometimes I think they need marriage more than we do."

"I liked being married," I said. "In fact, loved it—one man forever, well, at least till it fell apart. Then I got divorced and dated two guys, one right after the other, and I felt skanky."

Rachel smiled.

"Well, yeah, the sex was good, but there wasn't any love."

Then I dated a man I fell in love with and needed to back off. Was I commitment phobic?

"Sometimes we need time to detach, ya know?" she said. "Like with Nebraska football. We had those bad years and it was like somebody died. That's too invested. So, I've backed off. But then I've kind of latched onto Husker volleyball and started dating a guy…and he gets frustrated because I want to take it slow. Well, hell. I'm divorced and my friend killed my last boyfriend," she gave me a smirk, "and did me a big favor though I couldn't see it at the time. But Dan tries to push. Do you think it's because there aren't enough women out here? Maybe their breeding instinct kicks into hyper drive."

"Because there are more cows than women?" I said.

"Maybe so, but Jay left Omaha to come out here."

"Jay left Omaha, his job, his family, his home to be with you out in nowhere."

"Yeah, what's your point?"

It felt good to laugh.

"Anyway, we've been wondering about Buster," she said. "We've sent someone back up to double check on his whereabouts. He does have expired plates, but he does own the truck he's driving. We just gave him a warning on the plates. Jay, I mean Lieutenant Young, doesn't want to scare him away or make him think we're investigating him. And we're checking on his identification and everything else, but everything is moving so slow because of the holidays."

"There's going to be trouble," I said, as certain of danger as I was of my challenged height.

"You can't avoid Jay with all that's going on. What do you mean about trouble?"

"I'm holding up the life insurance payouts on two policies. If Val and Junior were killed for that money, then the killer should be getting antsy. Probate takes another couple of months at least. But the insurance companies can issue their drafts in a flash."

"We've been keeping an eye on the Percival house in Sidney, at least when Mitch is there."

"I heard. Speaking of trouble, I'm meeting Grant and Gage Redmond tomorrow. They are doing the electrical work on my new conference room."

She grinned at me. "Uh-huh. Stirring things up."

"And then, I'll be meeting Fred and Dave or at least Fred. One or both of them are crooks—they've been selling phony insurance policies. The state insurance department is investigating. I also called Robert Foxworthy to see if he knew anything."

"Oh, yeah, FBI in Denver. I think Jay's been in contact with him. And I've been keeping Tate in the loop. Funny thing, now that we're divorced, we get on just fine. He wanted the separation then balked at divorce. So I just went my way."

"He seems like a decent guy."

"Oh, he is, and a good cop. Though you spotted the flaw in the murder-suicide plan and he didn't."

"But he helped me get in the door and helped me to gather Mitch's stuff—that was a big deal for that boy."

"I finally saw him. He was on his way to school. What a sweetheart. Oh, and it turns out that Tate's boys know Noah and Ryan. So, now Mitch has two more protectors."

I nodded. "Hey, do you need a loaner from the library?"

"Mmmm," said Rachel as she rose out of the recliner and walked over to the book shelf. She tapped a thick, black tome. "Oh, yeah, I loved these Edgar Allan Poe stories—*The Fall of the House of Usher*, *The Tell-Tale Heart*, and *The Murders in the Rue Morgue*." She looked along the shelf then moved over to the other side of the fireplace and looked through that collection.

"This is just a sampling, I've got books all over the house, even down in the basement."

"Did you ever get a phone installed down there?"

I chuckled. "You bet I did."

"You know, I haven't read *To Kill a Mockingbird* since high school." She pulled the anniversary edition off the shelf.

"Hopefully, we can keep the mockingbird alive."

Wait, was there more than one?

Chapter 13

I arrived early at the firm, my body knotted in dread. Before I went into my office, I unlocked the conference room, our former garage. The duct work had been completed, so the room was as warm as the rest of the building. The locations for the electrical outlets were marked on the walls and ceiling. Later, Hank and Lew would add insulation, refinish the walls, apply wainscoting, wallpaper the upper portion of the walls, set up the mounts for the wall TV, and install the pad and carpet. At each end of the room were two wastebaskets where Brian and Rich played basketball with a dinky ball even I could palm. The job looked like it would only take a couple of days for the electrical work. Would it be enough time to get a feel for the two men?

Back in my office, I appeared to be working, yet my head and my guts were waiting for eight o'clock. Shortly before then, my staff began to arrive. Promptly at eight, I heard pounding at the backdoor. My stomach cart wheeled. I finished chewing my Rolaids then rose.

Out in the lobby, Gus was leading the two men back to the conference room. I jerked to a halt. My God! The sense of menace was so powerful, I struggled to breathe for a moment. Mom rushed from her desk to me. I'd only seen the men from the back, but they looked like Redmond men would look, tall and dark-haired.

She grabbed me by the arm. "Megan, what?"

"Evil," I said.

I waved Joy over to me as Melanie came near.

"Joy, I don't want your daughters coming here after school while those men are working here. Pick them up, and Kayla, too, and take them home, no, to my house. Patty will be there and you stay with them. I'll pay your time."

Joy looked alarmed, but nodded.

"Mom, call Patty and let her know."

Then I took a deep breath and walked into the conference room. As I introduced myself and shook their hands, my guts roiled and my heart thudded against my ribs. Yet the two men were cordial.

"So, what do you think…a couple of days?" I asked.

"Yeah, that's about right," said Gage.

Grant nodded then took his keychain out of his pocket and left the room.

"We'll try to get all our equipment out of the truck and in here so we won't be walking across your lobby," said Gage.

"Fine, I appreciate that." I said, now aware that in Grant's absence, the evil emanated from Gage. "I'm sure Mr. Werner told you that your day ends no later than five and you leave the premises every day from noon till one."

"Right, that'll be fine. I've been lookin' forward to eating at Custer's."

Back out in the lobby, I could breathe again. How I loathed being in that man's presence. What did it mean? I asked Glenda to take them coffee and her pastries. She said nothing. She'd never defied me before, but her eyes were big with alarm. I'd succeeded in scaring the staff.

"I'll go with you, Glenda," said Gus.

I nodded then went back to my office. Somehow I needed to function—my day was loaded with work and appointments. Yet before I forced myself to concentrate, I called Merritt and asked for a private meeting. He agreed to drop by my house after his shift. Then I called Chief Tate and asked that he or Deputy Bo swing by during the noon hour and a little after five to make sure the Werner Electric Company truck was gone.

Around ten-thirty, I caught a break and decided I would go check on the brothers. Grant was attaching a metal box to wires that hung from an open hole in the drywall. Gage was kneeling in the center of the room, sorting through a metal box of drill bits. I'm glad they didn't notice me at first—I needed to swallow my trepidation before I could speak.

"Ah, that Shiny Goblet's a faggot," said Grant.

"Hey, we don't use language like that in my firm, you son of a bitch," I said.

Both men looked over at me. Suddenly, Gage burst out laughing. Grant caught the joke when I grinned. He then smiled, but hung his head.

"So, what's the deal with Fred Goblet?" I asked. "Nobody ever has anything good to say about him."

"Oh, he's just a snake," said Gage. "There's a rumor going around that he's embezzling from his own insurance agency. I know he's got some bad debt…gambling, I think. He must need the money to get out of trouble."

Hmm. Embezzling? I doubted that, but it encouraged me that Gage would talk to me.

"This is a busy place," said Gage.

"Yes, especially right now. We're helping people get set up with the new health insurance plan. You guys probably have medical insurance through your company."

Grant nodded.

"And we're offering free living wills. If you guys don't have them, you should get them. Your mother is even coming out for one tomorrow. My dad wrote her will years ago. I've also learned some other things about your family."

Both men rose to their feet, their faces flushed with anger. Fear roiled in my intestines.

"Like the fact that most people think 1971 is a long time ago. But to you guys, I bet it still seems as vivid and painful as ever."

They stared at me. I deserved a blasted Oscar for getting that much out with my guts whipping around in a maelstrom.

"I'm sorry for your loss. My brother died, too. It seems so unfair. We know our parents will die before us, but we're supposed to grow old with our brothers."

In unison, the brothers nodded and looked down at the concrete.

"We know about you, too," said Grant.

I sighed for dramatic emphasis. "Sometime you should go see my horses. Strider and Rohan are in one of the pastures north of Harney Street over the noon hour."

At five that afternoon, I watched the Redmond brothers depart; they both stopped and told Glenda how much they enjoyed her baking. I said goodnight to Mom then went back into my office, closing the door. For the first time that day, I felt the air push deep into my lungs, as if I'd been taking half breaths all day long. The sense of evil and danger had been so clear. What did it mean? What did Gage do? It was evil, but when? Did it even pertain to the Percival deaths? No, I couldn't rationalize it away—it felt urgent. I wiped the sweat from my hands onto my worsted wool pants then dialed Jay on his cell. He answered immediately.

"Hi."

"Hi."

We'd shared more articulate moments, but this was hard and awkward for both of us.

"I'm meeting Sergeant Merritt at my house after his shift...which ends about now. I need to talk...about the murders."

"Okay. I'll be over. I'll need to come back here. We busted a guy who filled his back seat cushions with brown paper sacks full of pot. It was an easy bust because he was smoking some of his stash when he was caught. Rachel nabbed him."

"Good for her. I know she's working till later or I'd invite her, too. Um, okay, I'll see you in a bit. Do you need supper? Patty's making tacos."

"Oh, man, that would be great…otherwise it was a fast food burger."

"Okay, bye."

The day's sense of alarm morphed into a cloud of sadness. I wanted to be alone, didn't I?

Deputy Bo called to say the Werner Electric truck had headed back toward Sidney. I thanked him and roused myself to get ready for home. I called Patty to warn her that she'd be feeding more than me.

Patty had the taco fixings and a tossed salad ready for us. I invited her to stay and eat with us. Merritt said he'd only eat a couple as he was expected at home for supper. He ate five. The appearance of Jay made my stomach flip over—I hadn't seen him since Derek punched him in my front yard. I fought hard to eat, and push Jay and evil out of my mind. Merritt amused us with a story of playing Barbies with his daughter; that helped me get a taco down. The second taco started easier when I backed off the salsa and doubled the guacamole; still, I only ate half of it before I abandoned it in a crumbled mess on my plate. When I looked up, all three were staring at me.

"Megan, I've known you since you were twelve," said Patty. "What's going on? Do you need chocolate? I'll get some anyway."

While Patty was getting the chocolate, I felt the stares of the two men. Merritt's brows were scrunched tight together. Jay's eyes were big as he studied me. Patty opened a blue package then set it in front of me.

"Dark chocolate truffles from Belgium. I bought you ten bags." Then she sat down and waited.

I let the air fill my lungs then I said, "Evil. That's what I sensed today…and danger. I hired Gage and Grant Redmond to handle the electrical on the new conference room."

"I know those guys," said Patty. "They used to be troublemakers, though I haven't seen them since my divorce from Greg. Do you know which one is ah—?"

"Gage. The feeling was with him."

"Megan, I don't doubt you, but why?" asked Merritt. "He's not a beneficiary for anything. And there didn't seem to be any problems with him and either Percival brother."

"And Val would be his cousin, no, half-sister," said Jay. "He'd need to be evil to kill his own kin."

"Yeah, I know. It doesn't fit. Gage did tell me Fred was supposedly embezzling from his own insurance agency. But it doesn't make sense. Who would know outside of the agency? Fred's on the hot seat for selling phony insurance policies. But how does that involve Junior and Val?"

"Junior and Fred had a fight over something, but we don't know what," said Jay.

"Even Kenny doesn't know," I said.

"Do Gage and Grant know you're spying on them?" asked Jay.

"Well, hiring them was a way of meeting them. I'll have their work inspected, of course. And while Gage makes me want to vomit, I think I've befriended them." I looked to Merritt and said, "I learned a few things from dealing with Bert Bolger."

He nodded.

"I even have Granny Goblet, the former Lucy Redmond, coming out to the firm tomorrow."

"How'd you manage that?" asked Jay.

"Free living wills"

"Can't you get those off the Internet?" asked Jay.

"Sure, but they may not be Nebraska-specific. And people, especially the seniors, are always looking for a chance to socialize."

"So, you'll have the sons with the mother who left them as kids in your office at the same time," said Jay. "What time is her appointment?"

"Eleven-thirty. I bet she's planning to head to Custer's afterward."

Merritt indicated he needed to leave, so I walked the two men to the front door. When Merritt left, Jay turned and walked into the living room. Shit, here it comes.

I followed Jay into the room, resisting the impulse to fold my arms across my chest. I didn't want to come off as hard before he'd said a word.

"Why won't you forgive me?" he asked. "You must not care very much about me—it was so easy for you to dump me."

God above, why did you permit the Holocaust? Why do you allow men to be so stupid?

"I told you why. You hurt me so bad. You stirred up so much in me. First it was great then it was hell. I can't just flip a switch to make everything okay."

"So you won't give me another chance?"

"How many do you need to convince me you're not a screw-up?"

"A screw-up? No, I'm the man you want me to be."

"Are you? Are you worth the pain you've cause me? Your stupid blunder hurt me and that pain stirs up other pain—the deaths of my daughter, my brother, my father, and James. I hadn't healed from any of those losses then you come along and push me then injure me. Now those other wounds are bleeding again. I spent Christmas Day crying. Nobody is worth it."

"I know how Brian felt when you told him you were divorcing him. There's no persuading you."

"Why is it so terrible that I've decided having a boy-friend is just more than I can handle right now? I told you I needed some air. And you give me a week and here you are."

"You invited me."

"And the fact that you didn't leave with Merritt means you're selfish. You don't really care about me. You just want to possess me."

His face turned red. "That's not true. I care about you. I love you...I told you that. Don't you think the things we had, the companionship, the laughs, the loving, weren't those good things?"

It annoyed me that he argued so well.

"Didn't we share some things?" he asked.

"Yes, but you can't really understand me. You haven't suffered the things I have, so how could you really know me?"

"Megan, I want to try. Yes, you've lost so much, more than anyone I know. That just draws me to you. I want to be with you, even if it's just to cry with you. I can cry...you've proved that. How do you think I felt on Christmas? I was alone. I lost you and opened up a huge, ah, chasm, with my family. I felt like I'd lost everything. I listened to Leontyne Price all day then I remembered you said you like Luciano Pavarotti. So I listened to him and cried some more."

Oh! He was hitting me hard.

"It's just so much...grieving and being in a new love...it's emotional overload," I said. "And when something goes wrong—it really feels wrong. Stuff just keeps getting piled up and everything is amplified."

"Wait...you said 'new love.' So you love me?"

I looked down at the carpet. He took a step toward me. I stepped back. He stopped.

"Don't you think I could help you get through things?" he asked. "You know, help each other?"

"How does another person help grief? I mean, there's this huge guilt thing going on with Sweetie. Brian and I were both guilty and we couldn't get past that or didn't want to try."

"I don't understand what you mean about the guilt. You've never explained that to me, but I want to know. No, I won't have magic words to make it all better." He paused. "Do you want to be with Brian?"

"No. That love is gone...it died."

"Did you feel lonely when you were with me?" he asked.

"No, but you picked a bad time to screw up. If you didn't push me to go to Omaha, we'd still be together. I suppose life is full of what ifs. If Brian pulls the trigger he saves all three of us and I'm with my newborn, probably still on maternity leave and you're back in Omaha, dating that vixen."

"Yeah, what if. You know, you're pretty tough on people," he said.

"It's minimal compared to what I do to myself."

We both stared at the carpet.

After an hour or maybe a minute or two, I said, "You should probably go. I need to think about tomorrow."

He nodded and passed by me. I stood anchored to the carpet I no longer liked. I watched his cruiser head west on Harney Street. In time, I walked down the hall. I hadn't even heard Patty leave.

Chapter 14

ALL stirred up, I wandered the main level then stopped outside the study. I'd never read those letters from Val's roll-top. At the desk in the study, I took out the large envelope and looked through all of the contents, setting the letters aside. When I finally started to read them, I discovered they were from Pearl, her mother, who probably didn't own a computer. She possessed the handwriting of a senior, one who once thought good penmanship important, but now only managed jittery scrawl. Still, I could read it well enough to know it contained nothing more than the musings of a bored mother. I'd seen her at the funeral and knew she was a woman of medium height, who looked to be in good health; yet the horrible shock of her daughter's death had been etched into her countenance.

I shoved the envelope back into the desk. Those murders disturbed me. I started pacing again. Tomorrow, I'd be back at work with the Redmond brothers troubling me. God above, I needed to find a killer as nobody else had done so, but so many things gnawed at me, muddling my brain. I felt compelled to do something.

A few minutes later, I parked the Barracuda in the Percival driveway. The yellow tape was gone, but the house shouted its grisly nightmare. Hank or Lew had shoveled the last snow from the driveway, even though they accessed the house from the back. Once inside, I braced myself for the lurid agony I predicted the house still held. Junior's gasp caught me two steps in. I dragged the roll top desk into the TV room to get away from Val's screams. I probed every nook and cubicle, but found nothing of interest. The envelope of the papers I filched lay in the middle of the desk. It made me look guilty, so I removed the contents and set the pile of papers on top of the envelope. I closed the top then shoved the desk back. The north addition was still chained; Lew and Hank were making good progress. The drop ceiling was nearly complete and the walls were sanded down and ready for painting. The fireplace hadn't been installed and plywood still covered the floor as the carpet hadn't been delivered. I sensed a strange feeling that the murderer needed to be found and soon or—or what?

I walked through the laundry room-bathroom and out the other side into the master bedroom. I searched the drawers again. Nothing. I then looked through the nightstands, which I hadn't done before. In one drawer, probably on Val's side, I found a photo dated from 1995. Val stood next to a tall man; they wore summer clothes, looked trim, and smiled. This must be Buster, though only the date was noted on the back and a baseball cap shaded his face. I started to put it back in the drawer then hesitated. I shoved it in my purse. I could always return it or give it to Helen. The State Patrol had reviewed all the photo albums then released them to Helen, so this was the only photo they'd missed.

When my desire to depart the house of tragedy overwhelmed me, I hastened through the kitchen and front room, turning off the lights, and then welcomed the sting of the frigid January air.

Back home, I wandered up and down the hallway. The house of horror weighed heavily on me. Jay had crawled back under my skin. I couldn't think what would make me feel better. Bourbon? Nah. Yet another reading of David Copperfield and maybe some chocolate truffles with brandy? A few minutes later, I walked back to the family room with a bag from Belgium and a snifter of brandy. I conceded I'd never be able to concentrate on a book. When I sat down at the sofa, I spotted the gold envelope. Inside was a CD marked only with yesterday's date. When I put the CD in our DVD player, Toni Braxton's "Un-Break My Heart," filled the room. So, yesterday, he intended to persist. Would he after tonight's conversation? The song ended then Aretha Franklin belted "Until You Come Back To Me (That's What I'm Going to Do)." Okay, he's made his point. The next song was "Need You Now," by Lady Antebellum. I'd give him points for originality, but I didn't want to sit through a mishmash of sad songs. The final song was "Barracuda" by Heart. That made me laugh, though I already knew he had a fun sense of humor.

I sipped the brandy, but it made me think of James and the loss of him saddened me. Ah, hell, I needed to give in and go to bed. But I ate another truffle then said a prayer for Mitch's well-being; then I took another sip of brandy and prayed for myself.

Lucy "Granny" Goblet's arrival at eleven-thirty was a welcome distraction from the weight of evil Gage brought to the firm. Lord Almighty, how I hoped they would finish the work today. Granny, whom I called Mrs. Goblet, till she corrected me, was a frail-looking woman of seventy-five, with a curved, compressed spine, a thick waist, and skinny legs. She looked as if she gave birth to eight kids and they sucked the life out of her. Silver-rimmed glasses contained the thickest lenses I'd ever seen. I wondered if it was a good idea for someone with such impaired eyesight to drive. She quietly smacked her lips together whenever she wasn't speaking. I wondered if her dentures gave her trouble.

"I ain't seen you, young Docket, since you was still in college. Heard 'bout you lots. You caught them cross-burners…glad of that. Even better, I knew those Quinn women. You gave them peace. Your pa would be proud. I got me that glaucoma in my eyes. I take drops ever' night…lay in bed. Sometimes I barely get the cap on the bottle before doze off. I'm by myself. Ever'body moved out, got married and got kids. 'Cept Fred. That's best. And you got my two boys here workin'. They do good work?"

"Yes, I believe so. They were recommended to me. Of course, the county has to inspect, but it will be fine. Granny, shall we go over the living will?"

"Yep, yep. Got a bunion cut off last month."

I nodded. "Which foot?"

"Left. Good thing I ain't duck-footed like Pearl. She gets more and corns, too."

"She's coming out next week," I said.

"Oh, I'd like to see her. Always been a good friend."

I smiled. I wished I still had grandparents alive. At least I had Beulah. Granny nodded as she smacked her lips. I discussed the document then printed it. I asked Mom and Melanie to come into the office to witness it.

"Would you like me to send for Gage and Grant?" I asked.

"Oh, fine, good."

Melanie nodded to me, as I braced myself for their arrival. Evil walked in wearing navy cargo pants with pliers hanging from his side pocket. Grant followed then they both kissed her cheek and greeted her with "Mom." Where was the animosity? Did it die with Howard?

After I invited Granny to dine with me and my mom at Custer's, she said, "Yep, heard about all that with your folks. Gabby read the Dexter Gazette to me explainin' it all. Nice of you to forgive her."

"With God's help."

"Glad to hear you say that. I always think young people don't go to church."

"I think more believe in God than go to church. But it's good to expose them when they're young. Then they need to make their own decision when they're older."

She smiled and studied me. "You ain't like your pa. He'd never talk about this stuff...church and bunions...in his office. It was this one, wasn't it?"

"Yes. I moved in here after he died. It just seemed right."

A few minutes later, I sat in the Docket booth at Custer's next to Granny, facing the street, with Mom on the booth seat across from us. Gage and Grant took the table next to our booth. Beulah came by to chat.

"Well, I see you're still here, Blue," said Granny.

"Yep. You still in that big ole house?" asked Beulah.

"Oh, sure. Never get me outta there."

"Lordy, Lucy. That house got three flights of stairs."

"Oh, it's just me, so I just live on the bottom floor. Got a girl to help me with chores…comes twice a week."

Granny turned to Gage and Grant. "You boys go to church and take your families?"

"Yes, Mom."

"Yes, Mom."

She smacked her lips. "Good, good. You're good boys. You got good jobs…turned out good. Not like your pa, God bless his soul. That booze is bad, bad stuff. Turn a man into a monster. You don't drink, do you, Megan?"

"In moderation. Right now I'm more into chocolate."

"Oh, that's good stuff. And it's okay as long as you're thin. Do you exercise?"

Was she planning to adopt me as a granddaughter? Grant was grinning at me. Mom gave my foot a nudge. She was amused, too.

"Yes, ma'am. I keep at it."

"Yeah, that's my shrimpy girl," said Beulah. "Gotta go. Carol will be by for your orders lickety-split."

She gave us her Queen Anne wave as she shuffled away. Grant thought it was a hoot, though Gage had turned away to look at the front of the diner.

"Here's Buster, out on the sidewalk," I said.

The southern blinds were up as the day was cloudy. Granny squinted and looked toward the front of the diner.

"Yep, that looks like him, sorta," said Granny. "No, that's not him. Not so sure these days. Got that glaucoma. Put a drop in ever' night. Both eyes."

Gage had turned away and was talking into his phone. I looked out as Buster put his cell to his ear. Buster let go of the handle of the door and hastily turned away. What the hell? Grant looked back to Gage, bewildered. Gage silenced him with the shake of his head.

"Heh! Changed his mind," said Granny.

I looked down at my menu, trying not to alert Gage to the fact I'd noticed anything. We all ordered the Frank Docket Steak. Grant paid for his mother then he and Gage left as soon as they finished. Beulah came back to chat for a few minutes.

"Do you and Buster get along?" I asked Granny.

"Oh, sure. He calls me Lucy."

"Megan, Beth, do you gals want your desserts?" asked Beulah.

"Oh, you should box mine up for Granny to take home," said Mom.

"Mine, too," I said. "You take them, Granny. I get too sleepy if I eat mine. And I better get going. I have a one o'clock appointment."

"Oh, thank you, ladies," said Granny. "I think I might just stay a bit...have me some more coffee. I see Betty Finch over there."

We said our goodbyes and paid our bill.

When Mom got into the Barracuda she said, "Strange about her not recognizing Buster."

"Yes. Do not mention that to anyone."

She stared at me for a few moments then nodded.

At four-thirty, Celeste called, advising me that Buster visited and was on his way to my firm. I thanked her then went to Brian's office. January began the tax season blitz, first for businesses then later for individuals, so I knew he would be working late. Gage and Grant had finished their work and left an hour ago. That sense of relief disappeared.

"Hey," I said.

Brian looked up from his work. "How goes it? I've heard you're stuck in the middle of the Percival murders."

"Yeah, I represent both life insurance companies. Speaking of those, I have a person named Buster Redmond on his way. He is a named beneficiary on one of the policies. But, um, I'm not sure everything is quite right. He might be angry about something."

"I see. Do you have your gun?"

"Yes, but I don't think it's that bad. But would you open the door to him when he comes? I'll tell Glenda to get you. He doesn't have an appointment. Still, impulsive actions by former felons do worry me."

"Yeah, no problem. What did he do?"

"Assault and battery."

"Shit. I think I'll go warn Gus and Rich."

"Thanks."

I was talking to Glenda when Brian walked over to Gus's office. The tall, former linebacker should intimidate most people. Since our divorce, he hadn't been more than polite to me, but he recognized unusual circumstances.

A few minutes later, Brian opened the door to Buster. Rich stood talking to Melanie as a ruse and Gus suggested Buster take off his coat to hang on the overcoat rack. Buster looked at the three men then complied. As Buster walked toward me, Gus searched his parka, and Brian followed him to my office. After I greeted and shook Buster's hand, Brian asked if he should send Glenda in with coffee.

"I'll take one," I said. "How about you, Buster? And maybe a cream cheese Danish?"

"Oh, sounds good," he said.

We chatted about the duplex and he expressed his approval. Glenda brought in the refreshments.

"Now, what can I do for you?" I asked.

"I was just out to see Mitch. I think Kenny and Helen are good people, but Kenny is bit hot-tempered. I was thinking maybe I should be the executor for the will and the conservator for Mitch."

"I see." What was this snake planning? "Well, it's too late to be the executor because the probate process has already begun. As for the conservatorship and the guardianship, that petition has already been filed. And I think Kenny and Helen will do just fine. They know Mitch and his needs better than you, better than me."

Buster frowned, but said nothing.

In truth, I expected Judge Dean Shelton, a family friend, to reject the petition as Kenny was still a suspect in the murders. By filing the petition, I could prove that I was working to resolve the necessary legal hurdles. Also, the rejection of Kenny would be blamed on the judge, rather than on me. Once I received the rejection, I could re-file with Helen named as the sole guardian and conservator. This delay would allow the police more time to solve the crimes.

"So, now was there any life insurance?" he asked.

It was a natural question, but it raised my blood pressure. I doubted either Kenny or Helen would volunteer that information. What did he know?

"Yes, there is, but the disbursement of funds has been held up by the pending police investigation. This is an unusual situation, but most insurance companies are very conservative."

"You mean slow."

"I mean cautious."

"How much is the policy gonna pay out?"

"I'm not authorized to divulge that information. Again, the deaths by criminal acts do trigger an altered course of action."

"They just don't want to pay," he said with a scowl.

I shrugged. "I can't force them."

He took another bite of his Danish. He finished the whole thing in four bites. Is that a prison habit? Why did he make my bones nervous?

"Why don't you sue them for the money?" he asked.

"On whose behalf?"

"Mine…I mean…ah, I figure I'm a beneficiary on Val's policy."

"Why do you think that?"

"Ah, I'm just guessin'."

"I'm not at liberty to discuss the contents of the policy."

"Then let me read it."

"That would be the same thing. Unless you have anything else, I think this discussion is over."

He jerked to his feet. I hit the speed dial button for Brian then hung up. In ten seconds, the door flew open and Brian was in the doorway.

"Time for you to leave, Mr. Redmond," said Brian.

"Yeah, it's been a long day," said Rich from behind Brian. "I want to set the security codes and go home."

Buster glared at me then turned toward the door.

Melanie rang me. "You have another appointment, Mr. Fred Goblet."

"Send him in," I said then hung up. "It seems that I have another appointment. You remember Fred Goblet, don't you?"

When Buster turned back to me, he looked panicked. He then looked at the doorway. Brian now stood inside the door as Gus escorted the coatless Fred "Shiny" Goblet into my office.

I walked around my desk and shook Fred's hand. "It's nice to meet you, Mr. Goblet. You remember Buster Redmond, don't you?"

Fred stared at Buster for a few moments then smiled. "Why, sure. How are you, Buster? Good to have you back our way."

"Yeah, hi," said Buster. "I gotta get going." He hastened from the room.

What the hell?

Chapter 15

FRED looked like a Hobbit with the short, stout body, but without the hairy feet, I assumed. I offered him coffee and a pastry. Once he stopped watching Buster hurry out the front door, he glared at me.

"I want to know why the life insurance hasn't been paid. I know Kenny and Mitch are the beneficiaries of Junior's policy."

"So you sold the policy to Junior. But this one was valid...unlike some of the other policies you've sold. The insurance commissioner wonders who you've deceived."

Fred looked stunned—he didn't even turn from me till Brian escorted Dave into the room. He was slightly thicker than his brother.

"Hello, Dave. I'm Megan and I wonder if you sell phony insurance policies with your brother."

"What the hell are you talking about?" said Dave.

"Fraud," I said.

"You're crazy," he replied.

"The state insurance department doesn't think so, do they Fred? Or you can ask Aztec. I bet you used their name in some of the invalid policies."

Dave turned to Fred and said, "What's going on?"

Fred turned away from him and said to me, "You-you're just trying to hold up payment on the proceeds of that policy."

"Is a phony policy the reason you and Junior fought? There were witnesses."

"This is a trick—you're holding up payment," said Fred.

"Well, Aztec will never send that draft through you. Do you plan to tell Kenny you forced a speedy payment hoping to get a kickback?"

"Fred, we need to talk," said Dave.

"That sounds like a good idea. And Fred, maybe you can tell him why a book of matches from your favorite bar was found at the murder scene."

Dave's face slackened while Fred flushed hot with anger. He took a step toward me, but Brian caught him by the collar and turned him around. Fred looked up.

"I think it's time you left," said Brian.

Dave grabbed Fred's arm and yanked him out the door.

Dave turned back toward me and said, "I know you're friends with Celeste. I don't want her dating my son."

"I haven't talked to Celeste about her love life. She's more concerned about Mitch right now. And she'll be starting college in the fall on a scholarship. You look surprised. Maybe you don't know her as well as you think."

Dave huffed and left.

"You're playing dangerous games again, Megan," said Brian as he watched Dave leave.

"Thanks for your help," I said as I sat down at my desk and picked up the phone.

That's why we were no longer together—he'd help me if I needed it, but he didn't really support me.

Helen answered the phone. I felt obligated to let her know Buster's attempt to muscle his way into Mitch's funds. She thanked me and said she probably wouldn't let him visit anymore.

When I looked up, Rich was standing in the doorway.

"This place is stilled called Docket Law, but it's like night and day—a bit dull when your dad was here, he was all about business and only business. Someday, I'm going to come to work and there will be a ping pong table in the lobby. This place is like a fancy community center."

I chuckled. He was right—people stopped by just for Glenda's cinnamon scones, or for help on the new health insurance registration, or for help with their Medicare bills. My dad turned work away if he became too busy—I expanded by hiring more staff.

"But you're stirring things up," said Rich. "I told Gus I'd bet him twenty bucks you'd figure out who murdered the Percivals before the police did. He wouldn't take it." He chuckled. "I'll see you on Monday."

He left and I finally had a few quiet minutes to think. What did I now know? Gage Redmond was dangerous, but Grant probably wasn't. Fred Goblet was a crook, but Dave probably wasn't. Granny and her Redmond sons got along better than I'd expected from the stories I heard about that family, so Howard's efforts to turn his sons against their mother failed. Oh, and Gage and Buster had some connection, but it didn't seem to involve Grant.

Then Buster tried to take control of Mitch's finances—that didn't surprise me. Fred came to protest the slow payout of the life insurance benefit—that didn't surprise me. Fred's reaction to Buster—something was weird about that. He didn't seem to recognize him then he did. It all made Buster nervous. Was he thinking people expected him to look different because he'd been in prison? And then Granny Goblet's wishy-washy recognition of Buster—did that mean anything beyond proof of her poor eyesight?

Then another thought occurred to me—it was Friday night. Patty was going out with Paul Ritter, and Mom and Bill were headed to Kimball for a date. I would be alone; well, David Copperfield and I would spend some quality time together. This was the peace I'd been looking for—I should relish it.

On Saturday, Mitch came to see the horses. I went over to the barn early to make sure it was presentable—in other words, that it didn't smell too much like dung. Drew was there, sweeping the main floor. He tipped his hat to me. In the past, Jack and Bud had been my go-to cowboys for extra help with my schemes, particularly as members of the

Night Posse, the gang who helped me catch the scum who burned a cross on Rufus to intimidate James. But Jack had become Bill's number one man and Bud had left for college. Drew had worked for Bill almost as long as Jack.

"Hey, Drew, this looks really good. I appreciate this—isn't this your day off?"

"Yeah, but that's a'right. And no, don't think of paying me extra. I just want a promise—the next time you need back up or other help, call me."

"Do you have a gun?"

"Yeah, a Glock, something like yours. And a hunting rifle, of course, though I don't hunt much anymore."

"And do you know how to use it and not shoot off your foot?"

"Yes, ma'am. Jack told me you'd ask, so I got lessons and I've been to the firing range."

"Well, if Jack's giving you instructions, he must support you. I'll need your cell phone number."

"Okay, it ain't one of those fancy smart phones."

"Which are overrated, if you ask me. I have one and rarely use it for more than just a phone. I guess I'm not very techy."

While I was entering his phone number into my phone, Kayla entered the barn.

Drew quickly whispered, "I know she's too young to date. All the guys know."

I nodded to him as he lifted his hat for Kayla, which amused her. Car doors slammed shut. Ryan, Noah, Mitch, and Celeste entered the barn. Mitch stopped when he saw the horses.

"Who is that?" asked Drew. "She's of age."

"Celeste, come meet Drew," I said.

Noah and Ryan stayed with Mitch as Celeste came forward and met Drew. Mitch inched forward, his eyes big and his mouth slack as he looked at the horses. I walked over to Strider, my tall, jet-black stallion. Then I walked to the next stall and rubbed Rohan's neck; he was Brian's former horse, a beautiful palomino. Mitch took a step forward. I spoke softly to Mitch, telling him the horses' names, though I knew the boy didn't understand a word I said.

"Hey, Kayla got in trouble in school yesterday," said Ryan. "Go on, tell Megan."

"I kicked a boy in the shins," Kayla said. "I was walking with Mitch in the hall, and this butthead and his friends start taunting Mitch. I told the principal what the jerk said then I added that he said he was gonna put his hand down Mitch's pants to see if anything was there."

"What happened?" I asked.

"Nothing to me. The kid got detention."

"That's all?" I said. "That's not just bullying, that's assault to make a threat like that."

"Well, the last part was a lie," said Kayla. "I only said that because I thought I might get suspended or something for kicking him."

"Now, I don't condone lying, but that was probably a smart one," I said. "Still, he got off light. Maybe we should make an example of him? What do you think?"

Kayla smiled. She gave me his name and I called Rachel. After I gave her a rundown on the story, I hung up.

"That twerp will be getting a visit from both the State Patrol and the Sidney Police Department. That won't make his parents happy. So make sure you guys tell everybody you know at school that the cops are watching him."

Kayla high fived me and the others expressed their approval. Meanwhile, Mitch kept edging closer to Strider. When the tall horse swung his head toward Mitch he ducked behind me. I was the smallest one there, so I wasn't the best choice for protection. When I stepped closer to Strider, Mitch shadowed me. I could feel the boy's excited, hot breath on the top of my head. He was a mouth-breather.

"Eee-ooh," he cooed.

When I reached out to stroke Strider's forehead, a long, skinny arm moved beside my arm toward the long, black forehead. Strider sniffed the approaching hand, glanced at me, and then he dropped his head for Mitch to touch. I stepped in closer and Mitch moved with me. I ran my hand down Strider's neck and Mitch did the same. As Mitch touched the mane, a lump lodged in my throat. The room was quiet, even Rohan seemed interested.

"Eeee-ooh-eeeee."

Mitch, still standing behind me, moved his hand to Strider's ear, then quickly to Strider's large, black eye. Strider closed his eye and moved his head a couple of inches away. I firmly grasped Mitch's hand and moved it back to Strider's neck.

Mitch sang, "Whooh-ooo," three octaves lower.

"Ready to show off, Megan?" asked Drew.

I grinned at him. "Why not? I'll make it quick."

"Oh! Are you gonna show us the Ghost Rider?" asked Noah.

"Not really. That only works at night and when I'm in all black."

As I backed up, Noah put his hands on Mitch's shoulders and drew him back. I climbed onto the top of the wood stall door as Drew put the bridle and saddle on Strider, who bobbed his head and moved over to me. I slid onto the saddle and Drew handed me the reins. Drew cleared everyone back then opened the stall door then ran ahead to open the barn door. The cold air rushed in as Strider and I walked out into the yard.

When everyone was assembled at the door, I stroked his neck twice then pulled back on the reins. My steed performed to perfection—he reared up on his back legs and kicked his legs into the air to shouts and applause. I was relieved when he dropped to the ground, the big ham. It took all my strength to hang onto the saddle horn—I didn't fancy the notion of tumbling off his back. Seventeen hands was a long way down.

I led Strider back into the barn while Mitch, cooing something low, hid behind Noah. After I climbed off Strider and out of the stall, Mitch backed farther away from the horse. He stared at the horse in fascination then gave me a look I couldn't interpret. I invited the group to the house for hot chocolate and brownies.

A few minutes later, we entered the kitchen where the wonderful aroma of warm brownies called to us—to Mitch in particular, who had to be restrained by Noah.

"Oh, he knows what those are," said Noah, who then bent over and sniffed Mitch. "But first, Funny Guy, we need to take you to the bathroom."

"I'll get the Depends," said Ryan as he checked his watch. "It is his time. He probably got all excited by that horse."

As soon as Mitch was back in the kitchen, there was a knock at the back door. I went to let Drew in. He washed and removed his boots then joined us in the kitchen. He wore wool socks and jeans that weren't the baggy urban style, no cowboy would be caught dead in those, and a red flannel shirt. When his eyes went to the pan of brownies, everybody else stared at him. Broad-shouldered and ruggedly-handsome, his presence shouted: Man!

Noah and Ryan wanted to be like him; Kayla marveled at the sight of him; Celeste just plain wanted him. Drew walked over and stood next to her. I also responded to Man, but I required that he be an intelligent, educated, Christian version.

A few minutes later, we were all eating and drinking; meanwhile, Ryan placed himself between Mitch and the pan of brownies, he knew Mitch well. I walked up to Kayla, who was still ogling Drew.

"Some year, your time will come," I said.

She flashed a look at me then looked down in embarrassment.

"Just make sure he's the smart, Christian kind of guy."

She grinned and nodded then took a sip of her cocoa. I'd been taking her to my church ever since her mother died after a meth binge. The Ritters hadn't been regular church attendees, but Paul welcomed my interference. He'd even started joining us in the Harney Street pew at the Presbyterian church.

"Mom told us about Buster...how he was being sneaky and trying to go behind our backs," said Ryan as he gave Mitch a brownie but made him stand up tight to the sink to eat.

"Yes, he tried and failed. He'll never succeed, not while I live—and not even if I don't. I gave the county judge a call this morning...he's an old family friend...so he's been warned about that snake."

Celeste explained to Drew and Kayla her uncle Buster's relationship to the Percival family. I showed Kayla and Drew a photo of him on my cell phone. The sight of him soured my stomach. I now understood him to be a scheming maggot. How desperate was he? I sensed he was growing in danger. I looked at Mitch and his protectors. Was I in a room full of Mockingbirds? How could I protect them? And from whom?

So far Buster's alibi held; Rachel told me they went back to the rancher who hired him and he was certain Buster was in Cherry County on his ranch on the afternoon Junior and Val were killed. Gage was evil, I was certain of that, but of what? Was Fred more than a liar and crook? Was there someone else I hadn't met? Did the murderer really need to be a man? I'd been wrong about that before and it nearly cost me my life. What? Had I missed something?

"I said, we should get going," said Celeste.

"Oh, yeah, sure."

I walked them to the front door. Kayla said goodbye and walked across the street toward home.

"Oh, wait," I said.

I dashed to my study and got one of those stress-squeezee balls out of the desk drawer then ran back. I handed the purple ball to Mitch. He scrunched it and smiled, first at the ball then at me. My chest swelled.

"Weee-ooh."

"No truer words had ever been spoken," said Patty as the group loaded into Celeste's junker. "I wish a purple ball could make me that happy."

"And a big black horse," said Drew. "So, um, Megan. I haven't met Celeste's parents, er, father to ask, but what do you think about me asking her out?"

"She seems interested," I said. "I can give you her phone number. I should tell you I met her in jail. She was caught in possession of pot. But she seems to have mended her ways, especially now that she helps with Mitch. Oh, and she's interested in going to college next fall. She's taking classes at the Sidney community college right now. Then either Kearney or Chadron...so four hours east or three hours north."

"That's not too bad," he said. "Though she may not make it in that piece of junk."

Something was going to happen between now and then. I wish I knew what and where.

"Megan, you have that look," said Patty.

"Yeah, I have that feeling, too."

"Should I do something?" asked Drew. "I'm willing."

"I think you might be playing bodyguard...I just don't know for whom. Come have a bourbon with me while I think."

"That I can do."

Chapter 16

NOT long after I arrived at the firm for the day, I received a call from Buster.

"Um, I'm in a spot," he said. "I'm not gonna be able to pay rent. I'm gonna get a job and pay you, I promise."

"You told me you had money to get through the winter," I said.

"Ah, yeah, I did."

"But you don't have it anymore?"

"I'm gonna get some. Please don't make me sleep in my truck. It's cold."

"No, I won't. Keep in touch, okay?"

"Yep, I will."

"You're not planning to run are you?"

"Nope, I wouldn't do that. I'll call you when I get a job."

"All right."

What was going on? Did he lie to me about having money to pay for rent? I definitely didn't want him to leave until I figured out the mystery about him.

Pearl Redmond, Howard's widow, was early for her nine o'clock appointment. In her seventies, she had more spring in her step than Granny Goblet or most seniors. We worked out the living will details quickly, with a bit of chit chat. Then I asked who she wanted for an agent to make sure her final wishes were carried out.

"You," she said.

"But we just met," I said.

"I heard about James and how you stood by his wishes. I've also been talkin' to Beulah. She said you're the right one. And you know about hospice and all that. Look, my Val is gone and my son is never around. I can't rely on him."

I consented, though I didn't really want the task, then we finished the will with Mom and Joy as witnesses.

"May I ask you a question…um…about insurance?" I said. That wasn't smooth. "Let me clarify myself. Junior and—"

"And Fred were fighting…you heard about that." Pearl said. "That's because that sneaky Fred sold me some phony homeowner's insurance. Promised I could save a ton over my current policy…which costs a lot because of the storms we get. So I bought it. But I never got any paperwork after that. So I told Val and she was a good daughter…figured it out right away. Junior went after Fred, argued about it a couple of times, Val said. Meanwhile, she gets me set up with Allstate or State Farm or somebody reputable like that. Yeah, I lost money for the months I paid Fred…but didn't have any storms, so it was okay."

"I don't know if you'll get that money back. Fred will fight the accusations."

"Did that phony policy have something to do with why my girl and Junior were killed?"

"I don't think so. But yes, Fred is in trouble. He's been caught. And I don't think Dave was in on it. But if you still have any paperwork on that phony policy, you can give it to me and I'll make sure the authorities get it."

"Yeah, I just might. I'll look."

"Thank you. I do hate crooks."

She smiled and nodded. She dropped her chin into her best blue polyester jacket. For a moment, I thought she'd fallen asleep. Then she lifted her head and shook it till her wire rims slipped down her nose a pinch.

"Helen called me Saturday. Said Buster had tried to go behind their backs and get control of Mitch."

"Well, Mitch's money."

"But that don't sound like Buster. He's plenty rough around the edges, but not like that...he'd never hurt a woman or a child. He loved that boy."

She dropped her head into her chest again. I waited.

"I just don't understand it. Buster's been around here for a while they say and he's never been to see me."

"I heard he was in prison. Maybe he's ashamed."

"I don't care. I want to see my boy."

"Next time I see him, I'll tell him."

"I just don't understand."

She picked up the envelope, thanked me, and then turned and walked toward the door. I paused before I dashed after her to open it for her.

Now I understood.

I called Jay—I thought about calling Merritt or Rachel, but truthfully, I missed him.

"I can come over to your office at about ten-thirty, but then I need to get back for a meeting," he said.

"It's about murder. I don't want to deceive you."

"I'll see you in an hour."

When he arrived, he put an envelope on my desk.

"Oh, they're not a bunch of sad songs, are they?"

He chuckled. "No, don't worry." He sat down. "Okay, let's have it."

"Buster is not Buster," I said. "I bet he's a phony looking to collect on Val's life insurance policy. He even came to me to try and get control of Mitch's money...well, what he'd eventually get."

"Why do you think he's a phony?"

"Because Granny Goblet didn't think it was him. Then Fred hesitated when he saw him like he didn't recognize him...then played along."

Jay nodded.

"And he hasn't been to see his mother. But when I saw Pearl this morning, I knew."

"How?"

I took Val's photo out of my purse then walked around the desk to show him. It unnerved me to stand that close to him, but I tried to focus.

"This is Val and Buster about twenty years ago. He's lighter. And look at their feet."

Jay squinted at the photo. "They stand the same. They're duck-footed. I bet neither were great athletes." He took his reading glasses from his coat and put them on. "This guy is tall like the guy claiming to be Buster."

"But the man who claims to be Buster isn't duck-footed. The two men look alike, I'll say that. I bet he's a Redmond. Pearl was here this morning…I saw her walk. She's duck-footed like Val and how her son probably would be."

"I think you've got something. But we need to confirm it and find the real Buster."

"Well, that's all I have," I said.

Jay nodded. "The whole thing is still a muddle to me. And I'm the new boss and I get a double murder right off the bat and I haven't even made an arrest."

His phone rang, so he walked over to the window to talk. After a few minutes he came and sat down hard in one of the client chairs. I took the one next to him.

"Granny Goblet has been murdered," said Jay.

"What? God above! When?"

"Probably last night. Her daughter Gabriella found her just a few minutes ago. That was Merritt, he's at the scene."

"How did she die?"

"Someone broke into her house and bludgeoned her. A TV was stolen."

"Could that be a cover?"

"That's my thought. It was a mid-sized TV several years old. Not worth killing for." He looked at me, his face red. "Who kills a little old lady?"

"Only the deranged," I said.

I stood as he did.

"I better get going," he said. He stroked my cheek, turned, and left.

I sat down in my chair and stared intensely at nothing. My God, the depravity of the crime shocked me. Why?

Late that evening, at my request, Jay, Rachel, and Merritt gathered at my house. We sipped our bourbon in the family room.

"I have a few conclusions, no, guesses...if you want to hear them," I said.

"Fire away," said Jay.

"I think Gage Goblet murdered Val and Junior," I began. "He had access to the house and he knew their routine. I think he discovered the life insurance then stole page two of the life insurance statement from the roll top desk. I don't know how he escaped, but the man is evil. He wants to buy out Werner Electrical, but needs the money. I don't know how to resolve his alibi."

"Evidence is an issue, though it fits," said Rachel.

"I also think Buster is a fake. Granny, Fred, and Mitch didn't recognize him, and he seems unnaturally out of sorts with the Percival family. I think Gage hired him to play Buster. I don't know where Gage found him, but I bet he's a Redmond...the resemblance is close, but not quite right. Maybe he's a cousin. Maybe he has a different last name if his mother was a Redmond, but the father wasn't."

"I spoke with Robert Foxworthy this afternoon," said Jay. "The FBI thinks Buster stayed in Canada after he was released from jail. But he's been hard to track, taking only cash for his labor. He doesn't have a cell phone or an address that they've found. So it doesn't really track with the Buster that's here."

"And this Buster is suddenly poor," I said. "I think Fred has caught wind of the scheme. I bet he's blackmailing Buster, who stays in the area, hoping to still get some life insurance money. Fred could be blackmailing Gage, too. But he's playing a dangerous game with two villains. And I don't know why Granny was killed. What does her death resolve for anybody? And if he was the real Buster, why hasn't he visited his mother?"

"Because he doesn't want to be exposed," said Merritt.

"So, what if phony Buster killed Granny to shut her up?" I asked. "Were Fred and Gage in on the killing of their mother? You have to be a psychopath to kill your own mother."

Silence ensued. Did they think I was nuts?

"I bet you're right," said Jay. "But we don't have a shred of evidence to support any of your conclusions."

"I agree. It all fits if you think about the people involved…but proving it's gonna be tough," said Merritt.

"With Granny Goblet's death, everything has been shaken up," said Rachel.

"They're playing a deadly game that isn't over," I said. "Danger is so close I could choke on it." Oh, shit, I said that out loud.

"What do you mean?" asked Jay.

"I-I don't know…I can't explain it. But Rachel is right. Granny was the mother of eight people, seven living, plus grandkids. Someone will figure it out. I hope they go to the cops. Greg isn't in the area that we know of, but I've met all the others," I said. "Tomorrow, I'll make sympathy calls to the others now that I've met them."

"Megan," said Merritt who was looking at me sternly. "If you figure something out, don't go acting on your own. Call one of us—anytime."

"My new big brother is bossing me around," I said to Rachel, who smiled. "And he's right. But there are other people who need to be protected, especially Mitch and probably Pearl. Oh, and Rachel, and this has nothing to do with this stuff, but remember when we talked about me learning some self-defense? Maybe we should do that when you get a chance. Just not now after swilling bourbon. We'd fall asleep on the mat."

"Sure thing."

"Are you thinking you'll get mugged?" asked Merritt. "This isn't the Wild West or New York and you're not Kitty Genovese."

Rachel shook her head and rose. She and Merritt donned their coats and discussed their plans in the foyer while I took their glasses to the kitchen. When I returned, they left, though Jay lingered.

"You didn't ask me to help you with hand-to-hand combat," he said.

"Of course not. I can wrestle with Rachel and not want to tear her clothes off. My electricity doesn't flow in two directions."

He grinned at me. "So you still find me desirable?"

"That was never the problem."

"Don't you miss me sometimes? The way we talked and laughed..."

I downed the rest of my bourbon.

"You are disappointed in me. Well, I'm not happy with you."

"I have feeling you're going to tell me why," I said.

"You didn't rescue me."

"How's that?"

"That bitch drugged me and you deserted me. I needed you to come find me."

"Oh, that's so pathetic. You got played. Simple as that...and by someone you knew. You let that bimbo make a fool out of the both of us. And she's still laughing about it. And the fact that you dated such a conniving vixen doesn't earn you any respect from me."

"So I'm still a screw-up in your eyes. I got back to the hotel by six in the morning and you had already abandoned me."

"What was I supposed to think? Huh? You can't even say if you had sex with her. Have you had a complete blood work-up? She could have given you something."

"I'll get one." He went into the kitchen and poured himself a half a glass of bourbon. "My dad told me to chuck my ego and be prepared to grovel at your feet. And I am willing. But I've been trying to give you space. It's hard to grovel at a distance."

"Don't embarrass me."

He set a felt box on the kitchen table and opened it so I could see the gorgeous diamond pendant and matching earrings. Borsheims was written in the satin lining inside of the box.

"You can't buy my love," I said.

"It's a peace offering and an apology. If I could buy your love or devotion or fix this problem with jewelry, I wouldn't be interested in you. This is simply a token of my sincerity."

"It is gorgeous...I'll say that. And I did like your last CD—all those Josh Groban songs in Italian. I even looked up all the translated lyrics on the Internet. I do care for you."

"Has panic set in because you started to feel something for me? Megan, is this the easy way out of our relationship? Have you lost your courage?"

Had I? He poured me more bourbon.

"Maybe. I get scared too...scared of more pain."

"I know I pushed too hard. You warned me about that all along, but I didn't want to listen. Look, babe. Can't we just date? I'll take even one day a week." He took a swig. "I wonder if divorce has made you leery of commitment."

"Strange, but that's what I think about you. I mean, you're thirty-five, handsome, intelligent, successful, and you've never married. I wonder if you're ready to push till you've got me then you'll back off...scared of the responsibility, the obligation."

"That's not me. I know it sounds like a cliché, but I hadn't found the right person. Once I thought I had, but I wised up. You're the one for me."

He rinsed his glass and set it in the sink.

"Just think about it. One day…one day or night when we don't talk about murder." He turned toward the hall then wheeled back around and kissed me. "Goodnight."

Then he was gone, but my lips still burned and charges ignited and ricocheted throughout my body. I sat down on the floor. After a few moments, I stirred—a killer walked in my land. I scrambled to the front door where I found that Jay had locked the door on the way out. I set the deadbolt and the floor bolt, and then did likewise to the other doors.

One day. Granny Goblet murdered. His kiss. I sat down on the kitchen floor with my head in my hands.

Chapter 17

OF course, the report of Granny Goblet's murder was the big news in several counties. The next night, my gang materialized at my house. In time, I'd be on the hot seat. Meanwhile, Patty, Mom, and I prepared root beer floats.

"Patty, ah, how's it going with Paul?" I asked once I made sure no one was around to hear us.

"He's a good man," said Patty. "For the longest time I thought only an Indian could understand things. But I wonder about that now. Look at Vonny and Tony—they are doing fine, but a mixed couple would have a rough time around here. It's best that Derek married another African American if he was going to move back home."

"People don't really think too much about Indians and pale faces dating, don't you think?" asked Mom.

"Pale faces." Patty chuckled. "No, I guess not. And I am one-fourth German, though I don't think people remember that. But Megan, I think you're wondering about dating or not dating. I've spent long stretches in both situations. And a bad experience will make you want to do without. You need to give yourself time."

Mom looked around then said quietly, "Kayla is a complication, isn't she?"

"Yeah, I wonder if she approves, but I'm too chicken to ask her," said Patty.

"We've talked about it, but I don't think she knows what to think," I said. "You two were friends long before you started dating her dad, so that's in your favor. I did tell her that you were divorced and had been hurt more than once. So, you would be very cautious and decide things very slowly. I think she liked hearing that."

"The three of us have fun, but I'm not ready to be a threesome," said Patty.

The shuffling of clogs came down the hall. Beulah appeared in the doorway. "Oh, makin' root beer floats. Good, good. You got any of that fancy chocolate?"

"Oh, yeah. Try these," I said as I took a bag of dark chocolate truffles out of the cupboard.

"Mmmm! Those are good and I'll take one of those floats, too. That sugar will keep me going for a bit."

"I'm going to pass some of these out," said Patty as she loaded a tray with floats and headed toward the family room. Beulah shuffled behind her. Mom put her hand on my shoulder to stop me.

"There's something I've meant to tell you," Mom said. "Brian comes over in the evening now and then...once a week, I suppose."

"I think he always liked you better than me. In fact, you're probably the most reliable woman in his life. Think about it—his mother died, his daughter died, and I divorced him."

"He's suffering."

"I know, but I can't help him. He did everything he could to alienate me and he succeeded. If he regrets that now, well, it's too late. And more than that, we're just not well suited. It would have ended eventually. He thought he married Daddy's little clone, but he couldn't handle the woman that came out the other side. I've helped his career as much as possible. But right now, I've got my own problems and they don't include him."

She nodded.

"But I'm glad he has you and Bill. It's strange that he chooses to live in Dexter when most of his friends are in Sidney. I think he wanted to be Derek's buddy, but Derek's always going to be on my side. In time, he'll find the right woman and forget me."

She smiled at me and handed me a float. "Come on, hon, it's time for the inquisition."

I followed her into the family room. I sat down on the sofa next to Beulah with Mom on the other side.

"Just don't understand why Granny Goblet got killed," said Beulah. "People say her TV got stolen. Megan...Beth, did she say anything to you at the diner? She was talkin' to you two for a while."

"No, just that she has glaucoma," said Mom.

"And bunions," I said.

"But it doesn't make sense," said Bill. "That little old lady lives all these years then Junior and Val get murdered then Lucy gets murdered for a crappy TV. Megan, what do you know?"

"Know? I don't know anything. If there was something concrete, there would have been an arrest for the murders of Junior and Val, and for Granny."

"Yeah, but...you always have something figured out," said Bill.

"I'm the executor of the estate. That's my job. Yes, there are a few things I wonder about, and yes, I'm very interested, but I'm trying to stay out of trouble."

"Last night, three State Patrol officers met here," said Derek.

All eyes were on me.

"We were talking things over, but finding the killer is their job. Sticking my neck out just gets me in trouble."

"Best Friend," said Beulah. "There's truth in what you say...but you're also feedin' us some horseshit."

Patty burst out laughing, "Thank you, Beulah, for saying what we were all thinking."

Now I was mad. "Listen, the last time I got in the thick of things my daughter got killed and I nearly died. There is some real danger, some deadly force at work, and anybody not on guard is foolish. When you're out in public, keep your mouth shut and don't go spouting your opinions."

Dead silence.

"Did Granny die because she said something?" asked Bill.

"Or knew something," I said.

"Is the killing over?" Bill asked.

"No." I don't know how I knew that, but I was certain of it. I needed to leave, in fact, I wanted to bolt. "And no, I don't know who."

I was ready to spring off the sofa, but Derek anticipated my thoughts.

"Wait, we have something, well, Tina does," he said.

"Yeah, ah, we're going to open up a new restaurant," said Tina. "Dane Shuster, Beulah's nephew, and I have been plotting it. It will be in the old Pizza Shoppe building. Dan Righetti has agreed to work with us."

"He makes that great pizza," Patty said.

"He's a great cook, but he needed some help on the business side," said Derek.

"It'll be a pizza place meant to cater to a younger crowd," said Tina.

"Yeah, those youngsters get tired of old Custer's," said Beulah. "Need their own place, Dane says."

"So, pizza and pop is the theme," said Tina. "And kids like those sport drinks and fancy colored waters. We're not trying to step on anyone's toes, so no country music—we don't want to compete with the Cowpoke. We're thinking a fifties diner with chrome and neon lights and a fancy juke-box."

"As in more hip, less hick," said Patty.

"What's it going to be called?" asked Bill.

"We're still working on that," said Tina.

I began to relax, pleased with the change of subject.

"Dane wants to call it 'Tina's,' but she objects," said Derek.

"I think it's good," said Beulah. "It don't sound hay-seed."

"How about Dexy's," I said. "As in Dexter and rhymes with sexy."

Silence. I guess that was stupid. I should have left.

"That's awesome," said Kayla, who sat on the floor by her dad's chair.

"Oh, that's good," said Tina. "And if the place fails, we can blame it on some anonymous character."

That brought chuckles and the chance to head for the kitchen and chocolate.

The desire to bolt stayed with me into the next day, but it was January in the Nebraska panhandle, which meant blistering gusts and wind chills below zero. Still, when I got the chance the next morning, I drove out to Hexam Road. One of the cowhands cleared the east-west road in the northern section of our family wasteland. I parked just south of the Joker, a bluff with a strange indentation on the west side that made it look like it had a wide-open mouth. Once, I climbed up there and waited for God to strike me dead for my sins, but it wasn't on his To Do List that day.

As I stared out at the bluff, my heart started to thud against my chest and my guts commenced churning. What now?

A State Patrol cruiser pulled up behind me. My breathing became easier. Jay trudged through the snow to the Barracuda then slid into the seat.

"I went to find you at your office, but you were just pulling out of the parking lot so I followed you. Remember that call to the FBI you made? It wasn't in vain. I've been talking to Robert Foxworthy. They've been searching for Buster. Nothing yet, but they're on it. I guess I didn't really have anything to tell you."

I told him about Dexy's. He seemed interested.

"That sounds great...and I'm so ready to hear about positive diversions. I can't sleep, my mind is so knotted. You're right about it all, but proving it is hard. I'm getting pressure to solve something or at least make an arrest. But I refuse to arrest Kenny just to placate the bosses."

I could barely hear him with the blood thudding in my ears.

"Megan, please talk—"

I whipped off my seatbelt and lunged at him. I wrapped my hands around his neck and pulled him toward me. He came easily. I kissed him then was forced to pull back to breathe.

"Something. Something soon."

"What? Babe, what are you feeling?"

"Frightened." I closed my eyes and tried to clear my mind. "What time is it?"

"Eleven-twenty."

"Can you come to Custer's with me?"

"Sure. Why?"

"I don't know. Oh, hey, have you talked to Buster about where he was when Granny was killed?"

"He says he was at home. A neighbor says his truck was in the driveway that night and a light was on in the front room."

"He has a garage," I said. "Why would he leave it in the driveway at night?"

"So that someone would say he was home."

"Any stolen cars in the area? Smokey's lot may have a truck missing."

"I'll check."

"Okay, follow me," I said.

Jay went back to his cruiser. Why does he or anybody obey me? I'm probably nuts.

I parked in the lot behind Custer's like normal. Jay parked next to me. We walked in the front door together and sat at the Docket booth. I called Mom to tell her I had arrived. I tried to drink a root beer, but the fizzy sugar made my stomach turn over. Beulah scrunched her brow at me.

"Hot tea?" she asked.

I nodded. Mom arrived a few minutes later.

"Patty's on her way," she said as she slid into the booth. "What's up?"

I shook my head. Jay, who sat next to me, glanced at my hands, which were latched tightly onto the table so that my veins were popping up and my knuckles were white. The door opened and the phony Buster walked in. He glanced over at me and Jay then sat at the counter. Then I knew, but it was too late.

Patty walked in the front door. She glanced over at the phony Buster, who turned in his chair to look at her even after she sat down next to Mom.

Shit. Oh, shit.

"Patty, you saw that man at the counter—don't look over. Is that Buster Redmond?"

"No, it's not, Megan. He—oh, God. That's the guy who says he is. Greg and I used to spend time with Buster. That guy is not him."

"Okay, here's what we do," said Jay. "Patty, I'll take you back home, er, to Fort Docket."

"Patty, I'm going to go over and talk to him," I said. "You go like you're heading to the restrooms. When he's diverted, you go into the kitchen and out the back door. Jay will meet you in the parking lot and follow you home in his cruiser. Mom and I will stay here and attempt to eat. Then we'll figure something out. Just stay at the big house. I'll call Derek so he knows."

"You're good at this," said Jay to me as he slid out of the booth and left for the front door.

"Wait, hang on, both of you put Jay's cell number in your phones so you can call him quick." After they entered his number, I said, "Okay, he should be back there. Patty, go, but not too fast."

I slid out of the booth and Patty walked at a normal pace, looking straight ahead as I walked over toward the counter. Phony Buster watched her until I came up on the other side of him. For a moment, my throat constricted. Patty was nearly at the back of the diner. I needed to distract him. Quick breath.

"Hey, Buster, how goes it?" I managed.

He turned toward me. "Wha? Oh, fine."

"You do need to come up with the rent money, but I understand everybody has tough times." I forced my eyes to stay on him, don't look away, don't give her away, don't do it.

"Ah, yeah."

"Beulah, give Buster a Frank Docket Steak on me."

She nodded, but studied me hard. When Buster turned to her, I could look past him—Patty was out of sight.

"Have you checked the brewery? That root beer was created by Beulah here. Yeah, that's her concoction. They may be looking for help. It's just southeast of town. Good luck."

"Ah, thanks, Megan."

As soon as I walked away, he looked to the back of the diner then to our table. Mom played her part well, keeping her eyes on the menu while phony Buster was looking around. Mom and I ordered, though we both struggled to eat and to find trite conversation to occupy us. A few minutes later, I got a text from Jay, telling me that he and Patty were safely at my house. When I showed it to Mom, her tightened shoulders relaxed.

When I got back to the office, I called home. Jay said he could stay till one-thirty. I called Derek, who said he'd go over to our house with Tina and his dad's shotgun. Then I called Bill requesting the services of Drew with the promise that I'd explain everything to him later. My next call went to Drew. He agreed to head over to my house armed and with the password "Pooper's Canyon." I called Derek back and described Drew to him so he'd know he was the next shift. As I expected, he laughed at the password.

"I expect you to tell me everything," he said.

"I will...later, but don't bother Patty with questions right now."

Patty, my Patty, who had been my nanny, friend, protector, counsel, housekeeper since I was twelve, was now in extreme danger. I would do anything to protect her. I called both insurance companies and told them to continue the delay on issuing the checks—with Aztec, I told them Kenny, a beneficiary was still a suspect in a murder; with State Farm, I told them that Darold, a beneficiary was now a suspect in a murder, though I didn't specify which murder. I felt certain the phony Buster killed Granny. Should I have anticipated she would be in danger? I wouldn't make that mistake again.

Chapter 18

HAVING attended to all my appointments, I left work early. I called Jay to recommend a big meeting of protectors. He suggested we meet early to discuss things. When I arrived home, I discovered people were ready to protect Patty. Derek and Tina sat at the dining room table working on their laptops. Kayla sat at the front window on a dining room chair with her laptop on a pillow on her lap.

"Hi, gang," I said. "I'm sorry about this. I know you have things to do."

"Miggy, that's the last apology I want to hear from you," said Derek. "We know Patty's in danger. We're ready to help."

"We insist on helping," said Tina. "Derek has always raved about her cooking. We're amassing a collection of her recipes."

"I've been making her chicken parmigiana for years," said Derek, whose shotgun lay on the floor behind him. "And we know we're going to find out more. I bet you're planning a meeting for tonight."

"You know me well," I said.

"And I know your sense of protectiveness."

I smirked and turned to Kayla. "Now what are you up to? Are you waiting for the corn to grow?" I said in reference to the snow-covered field across the street.

"No, you goof. I'm recording all the cars and trucks that pass by. When I came home I saw Derek and Tina come over here and Derek with his shotgun, so I followed them. Now I'm making this list...it was Tina's idea. Then Derek showed me how to look up the make and model. I guess I don't really know cars."

"What a smart thing to do," I said. "Thanks, guys."

While Tina was showing me the logo for the Dexy's sign, Kayla jumped up.

"That white car, uh, Ford sedan has been by here twice now, both times going east. It's slowing down, now going west."

In a flash, Derek, grabbed the shotgun and ran outside to the sidewalk. The car lurched forward then sped toward the highway.

"It went north," said Derek as he dashed back inside the house. "It's bloody cold out there. The license plate was too muddy to see the numbers, but it was a Nebraska plate."

"Bloody?" asked Kayla. "Do you watch the Harry Potter movies?"

"We love 'em," said Tina.

Kayla sat down with her laptop. "Let's see, is this it, a Ford Crown Victoria? Hard to tell the year since they didn't change much in the nineties. Let me see if I can find a white one."

We all looked at her laptop.

"Dang, that's it, Corporal Kayla," said Derek. "This is stuff cops do."

"And I took a picture of it on my webcam. Let's see if it looks any good." She hit a few keys.

"That's not bad," I said. "Good, considering you had to hold it up in the air to photograph it. We better not tell the State Patrol. Jay complains that their recruitment numbers are down."

Derek and Tina were still laughing as I left to inspect the rest of the house. Mom and Patty were preparing hamburger patties for an unknown number of people who might show up hungry. As soon as I walked in the kitchen, Patty handed me three truffles.

"I've been going at 'em, too," said Patty. "I'll confess, I'm good and scared."

"I'm not going to let you get hurt," I said then I gave her a hug.

"I bought a ton of ground beef," said Mom. "Earl Ferdy is convinced were planning to feed the town."

"Hey, what was Derek doing?" asked Patty.

"A car slowed down in front of the house, so he ran out with his shotgun to scare them away. And Kayla is listing all the vehicles that pass by. We're all going to need Rolaids for our stomachs and beta blockers to handle our skyrocketing blood pressures."

"Glenda sent the rest of the day's scones home with me," said Mom. "And she gave me the stash she keeps in the freezer in case of emergency."

"So they know something is up," I said.

"Yeah, everybody knows how to read the both of us," said Mom. "By the way, do Gus and Rich know how to use guns?"

"No, they're normal. But that reminds me, I need to let Brian know what's going on. He was in Sidney all day."

I called him from the kitchen phone and gave him the scoop; I even invited him to our meeting. He was appropriately concerned. He promised to stop by Cabela's and buy extra ammo for our matching Glocks. I agreed, though I didn't really need it. I'd only fired a few bullets outside of the firing range.

I proceeded to the family room. Drew was laughing at *Monty Python and the Holy Grail* from the recliner. He had a handgun on the end table next to him and a rifle set up against the wall near the door. I greeted and thanked him then watched the Black Knight get his appendages cut off as he taunted King Arthur.

"Derek brought over his dogs," said Drew. "He brought them inside a few minutes ago. That beagle puppy, ah, what's his name?"

"Trotwood," I said.

"Yeah, he gets cold fast. So Derek's been runnin' them in and out of the house. The pup pesters Barnaby constantly. I think Barnaby likes it, but he gives the pup a nip now and then."

I went back to greet the back door guards, who were confined to the mud room and rear hall with a door gate. Those dogs would know if a stranger approached the back of the house. All our meeting members would need to go greet the dogs so the pooches knew who were considered friends. Harney Street also had Bill's lab, Traddles, and the Ritters' husky mix, Boo. I played with the dogs for a few minutes then walked down the east hallway and washed my hands in the bathroom next to the study.

The doorbell rang. I found Jay waiting for me in the living room. I took him to the study and gave him the rundown on our preliminary precautions.

"Anything more on Granny?" I asked.

"No, it was a simple, brutish break-in and murder, probably with the blunt side of the axe found in the back yard," he said.

"It's so different than the Val and Junior murders," I said. "Those were well-planned...so maybe we have two different killers."

"The second murder was probably done in a hurry so careful planning wasn't possible."

I nodded. "I still think Gage killed Val and Junior, and then phony Buster killed Granny to prevent her from claiming he wasn't Buster."

"Who has disappeared."

"What?"

"He parked his truck in the driveway of the duplex yesterday and hasn't been back. All personal belongings are gone."

"I knew he'd stiff me on rent."

"The FBI has identified him as Roger Harper. He's an illegitimate son of Howard Redmond, which is why he looks like a Redmond."

"So not only was Howard beating his wife and sons, he was screwing around. What a pathetic excuse for a human."

"This Roger Harper has his mother and other relatives on the Pine Ridge rez, though we think he has spent time on the Rosebud rez north of Valentine."

I nodded.

"Damn, you said he was a phony. I should have arrested him."

"On what grounds?" I asked. "His ID checked out till now. You can't arrest people based on my theories. I think Gage killed Junior and Val, but we can't prove how he did it."

Jay plopped down into a chair then rested his head against the wall.

"Okay, this is what I'm thinking," I said. "We have this meeting to delegate protection duties. I've called some people and so have you. We should have food for whomever needs supper or snacks...and plenty of alcohol, of course."

"Of course," he said with a smile.

"And root beer and vanilla ice cream."

"Of course."

"We'll have two cowboys, Jack and Drew. Bill will give out information to his other cowhands and put them on alert. Just make sure the cops you send over here know that we'll have armed cowboys in the area. They're on our side if they're wearing cowboy boots that smell of cow dung."

Jay smiled.

"Okay, stand up, please," I said then closed the door quietly.

I walked up to him and pressed my chest against him and wrapped my arms around his back. He returned the hug, but said nothing. I let go after a half minute—I didn't want to get him too excited. We both needed to concentrate.

"Thank you," I said. "I needed that for my blood pressure. The chocolate truffles didn't help. Hanging out with the dogs did seem to make me feel better. They're funny and simple and didn't ask me any questions. And no, I'm not feeling amorous, just scared, but to everybody else, we need to look like we're in control."

"I never thought of it before, but you're a very physical creature…I mean you're other things, too, but yeah, sex, food, warmth, touch…you're very responsive."

And wind. I respond to it, too, and its gust was ominous right now.

"Uh-huh. So you lead the meeting and I'll chip in here and there. We'll feed people then meet in here. We can set up a few chairs, others can stand. This will become the War Room again."

"Again?" he asked.

"This is where my crew gathered to solve the Quinn murders."

"Right. And you found the answers in the law files. I may be requesting those for the involved families."

"Okay," I said.

"That was easy. I thought you'd protest that. Oh, got it. You've already copied and read them. Did you find any-thing?"

"Unfortunately, no. File information helped solve the Quinn murders, but it hasn't helped in this mess. I'll look back through them for any reference to Roger Harper, but I don't recall seeing that name."

Jay walked around the desk to look out the window. I sent an email to Melanie to get her searching public and legal records tomorrow for anything regarding Roger Harper. It was a long-shot, but I wanted to cover every base.

Soon, the house began to fill. I spotted Drew talking to Kenny in the living room. Kenny looked bewildered by Drew's old-fashioned request to date his daughter. Kayla stayed by the front window, though I suspected that she was eavesdropping on them. Tina showed Rachel and Paul plans for Dexy's on her laptop. Ryan and Derek intently stared at Derek's computer screen. Meanwhile, Beulah wandered around the kitchen eating chocolate with Linda,

Lew, and Hank. Jack and Merritt narrated the exploits of the Night Posse to Johnny Two Rivers, Chief Tate, and Trooper Jim Loske.

In time, anyone who wanted a burger and a salad finished then we distributed desserts. Brian, Drew, Ryan, and Derek began bringing chairs into the study. Even though people seemed chatty, tension shrouded the group in an invisible cloak. Nobody walked by a window without looking out; rifles were placed by the doors and windows; and every one stopped to study Kayla's list of cars and trucks.

As people gathered in the War Room, a somber hush fell upon the occupants. Merritt set up two by three foot poster boards of Mitch, Pearl, Patty, Roger, Grant, Gage, Fred, and Dave photos.

"Welcome to Fort Docket," I said. "Lieutenant Jay Young of the State Patrol will discuss the status of the crimes that have hit our communities. As you can see, we have several photographs placed for you to view. On the left, we have Mitch, Patty, and Pearl—people we think may be in danger and need to be protected. On the right are faces of people who may have some knowledge or guilt in some of the recent wrongdoings." I looked over to Jay.

"First off, this photo is of a man who has been going by the name of Buster," said Jay. "His name is actually Roger Harper, who has recently disappeared and is considered highly dangerous."

People began to murmur.

"Has anyone seen this man in the last two or three days?" asked Jay. "If anyone sees this man, do not hesitate a moment. Call the police."

Rachel began passing out a list of phone numbers for various police officers. Jay covered the plans for an ongoing rotation of troopers and police department officers at the three homes.

"The task for most of you is to be alert and report anything amiss. Bill Docket and Joe McCready will be putting their staff of cowhands on alert. Besides the rotation of police, I would like volunteers to serve as bodyguards. You need to legally own a firearm that you will keep with you. We don't expect twenty-four hour service, but any help is appreciated."

Drew raised his hand. "I can be available after work hours. I have a sleeping bag and a handgun and a rifle. I'd like to sleep indoors."

"Heh! Wouldn't we all!" blurted Beulah, to chuckles that eased the tension in the room.

Kenny raised his hand. "I'll take that young fella to help guard Mitch. And I would like to make a request. I do own a rifle that is in Junior's basement…so, ah, I would like access to it. Otherwise, we don't have any guns in the house."

"I'll discuss your request for the gun with you after the meeting," said Jay.

Jim Loske raised his hand. "My wife works till midnight, but is willing to stay wherever she is needed. She will require a bed."

"Heh! She's a wimp," chimed in Beulah to more chuckles.

"Pearl's house would be a natural place for Marty since they'd both be in Sidney," I said. "Otherwise, we'd take her."

"I think the Sidney police have started full-time day coverage for Pearl, so Marty could pull the night duty," said Rachel. "I'm willing to stay here after my day shift."

"Actually, I'm going to assign your day shift here, Officer McNeill," said Jay, "at least for the next few days."

"I can cover evenings here," said Jack. "I'll chance the weight gain."

More laughter followed, the nervous kind from people who knew lives were in danger. I nodded to Jack.

"I'm at home," said Derek.

"I can come over," said Paul.

"No," I said with a bit more harshness than I meant. "You have a young daughter. Leaving your home makes

LIES IN THE WIND

you vulnerable. Bill, Derek, Paul, you are more valuable as lookouts, and you also have dogs, who are the best lookouts. The areas around your houses provide natural hiding places. The same goes for you, Hank, Lew, and Linda. We need your lookout."

Heads nodded.

"What about Mitch's ride to and from school?" asked Bill. "Seems like he could be vulnerable."

"I could check with the sheriff, but we're getting stretched thin," said Jay.

"Kenny, would Helen be able to drive Mitch to and from school?" asked Bill. "If so, I'll contribute Drew to ride shotgun." He looked over at Drew, "With pay."

"We've been talkin' about it," said Kenny. "Helen is willing, so that would be great. I think all of this is really kind of you people. And Mitch has been around Drew some, so that's good."

"So, which of these guys should we be looking for?" asked Derek.

"Any of them, but Roger is the biggest threat, we believe," said Jay.

"How long do we expect this to go on?" asked Paul.

"Hard to say," said Jay.

"It'll happen fast," I said then I wished I hadn't.

"How do you know?" asked Chief Tate.

"Just do."

"Heh! Don't you be doubtin' Megan…none of you," said Beulah.

I smirked at Beulah.

"Okay, thank you, folks," said Jay. "Call us if you have any questions. Oh, and these arrangements should start right away. So, Kenny, Mitch should either be at school or at home."

"That's what he likes," said Kenny.

"And you mean I need to stay here every day, all day?" said Patty. "Well, that's kind of like the last twenty years of my life."

People laughed as they began to disperse. Kenny and Ryan moved off to the side to wait for Jay.

Jack, Merritt, and Rachel were soon beside me.

"So, fast you think?" said Merritt.

"Yeah, I do," I said. "These are big crimes for people who aren't hardened criminals. Roger cudgeled Granny out of panic. And it just feels like…more…soon."

"More? Good God, Megan," said Merritt.

"We've had enough, I know."

Jay walked over to Kenny and Ryan and my group joined them. I waved Drew over.

"That's a tough request," said Jay to Kenny. "That means removing a weapon from a crime scene."

"The police may not be able to help you, Kenny," I said, playfully and literally elbowing my way in front of Jay. "But Drew has that rifle, right? And you have a license for it, right?"

"Yes, ma'am," said Drew.

"And Kenny, you have a license for firearms, right?"

"Yes, I do."

"Okay, then, Kenny and Ryan. When Drew has to leave, he takes his handgun with him and leaves the rifle in the house. And if someone there needs to use it, so be it. And that's not coming from the police. Got it?"

Jay chuckled behind me. Rachel started laughing.

"I didn't hear anything," said Merritt.

Kenny smiled. "Got it."

"So are you a decent shot with a rifle?" I asked.

Kenny shrugged.

"Never mind. Ah, so Officer McNeill is here during the day tomorrow. Officer Merritt, would you have the opportunity to come by here about four in the afternoon? I've never learned how to use a rifle. I think I ought to know. Maybe I'll buy one. And while you're teaching me, if some others wanted to come by while Drew is with Mitch, then they could, right?"

I was surrounded by smiles.

Jay's arm came from behind and wrapped around my neck. "This woman has corrupted my officers and local citizens, all in the span of a minute."

"Well, don't stop her," said Rachel with a wink to me.

"Yeah, I don't really need to catch any drunks or smugglers right then," said Merritt. "Four o'clock."

Chapter 19

A S the group cleared the room, I drew Merritt aside. Jay and Rachel followed.

"Is there any connection between Kenny and Gage, or Helen and Gage?" I asked.

"I wondered about that," said Merritt. "But it doesn't look like they were anything more than acquaintances. Kenny said he uses a Sidney electrician for anything he can't do himself."

"And I wanted to ask about Gage's alibi for the day of Junior and Val's murders."

Merritt drew his notebook out of his pocket. "He left for the day just before Hank and Lew did. Hank and Lew confirm that Gage had completed his work on the project and he did not return that day. Neighbors confirm the Werner Electric truck left then and never returned. The company secretary, er, assistant, said Gage arrived at the office just before noon. Gage and Grant were both there when her shift for the day ended at one o'clock. After that, Grant states his brother was on the premises. Grant says he went home about eight and his brother was still in the shop."

"That's a long day," I said. "Where's Mr. Werner on that day?"

"He works only in the morning, as he did that day."

"Do they normally work that late, especially when Gage has just completed a job?"

"Grant said they did work late that day...later than normal. He said he took a quick nap after lunch, but he doubts Gage did. Gage brought fast food burgers on the way back to the shop from Dexter."

I folded my arms and started pacing the room.

"What are you thinking?" Merritt asked.

"I'm just trying to figure out how Gage did it...I'm certain he did. And he hired Roger Harper to play Buster."

Heads nodded, but nothing was said. I felt frustrated, but clueless as to the next step.

"I'm going back to the office," said Jay.

"I'll be here at eight," said Rachel.

I walked with them to the front door. Sitting on the foyer bench was a stack of papers, which I glanced at then handed to Jay.

"My mom took notes."

He grinned.

Patty came around the corner. "Jack said he'd grab his stuff and be back in twenty minutes. So what's the plan? Should I just sleep in the guest room?"

"No, I want you in my dad's old room, right across from me," I said. "Jack can sleep in the guest room."

"Ha! You won't be much of a protector, Megan. You sleep like you're dead."

"I don't think it'll be that way, even with the bourbon I'm about to drink. Any takers?"

"I refuse to incriminate myself while my boss is here," said Rachel.

Merritt smiled.

"Okay, I'm leaving," Jay said.

He did get in one glance at me that said he wished he was staying.

I wanted him to stay. Wait—did I just think that? I'd wanted him to stay away because I needed time and peace. Well, forget about peace while Patty was in danger. She stayed up and drank with me, Merritt, Rachel, and Jack. I did feel better while they were around, but the sense of alarm and foreboding made my guts roil. After the cops left, I downed several Rolaids, which didn't help, so I ate some toast, which did, and then helped Patty and Jack get comfortable for the night.

During the night, I awakened from a dream about contour maps. I studied those in my college geography class. What the hell? Contour maps. Squiggly lines on hills and mountains. Then I knew. Jay liked to wear skimpy, satiny underwear when we were still dating. Red, royal blue, black—they'd been his signature and I loved them. Then he discovered stripes—white and black with pinstripes. Unlike school maps, these forms moved and the contour lines shifted and stretched and burst off the page. Oh, how was I supposed to sleep now? Emotional entanglement—did I want to chance it? I turned off the electric blanket and rolled over to a cooler spot.

In the morning, Patty fed Jack a huge breakfast. Once Rachel arrived, I left for work. Derek set up stakes to tie the dogs to at the edge of our backyard. A couple of pickup trucks were parked in the street in front of our house. Bill must have ordered a couple of his hands to park there.

At the office, my first arrival surprised me.

"I'm sorry, I didn't make an appointment, but they said you had some time open," said Fred Goblet.

"What can I do for you, Fred?" I had no idea what was coming—maybe a denial of some sort.

"Um, I need to hire you to represent me on the insurance fraud," he said.

"Now, Fred, you know I can't do that. I represent an insurance carrier who does business with your firm. It would be a conflict of interest. I think you know that."

He looked down at his hands in his lap. His jaw muscles worked hard as he clenched his teeth. This man was afraid. I got up and sat down in the client chair next to him.

"You've gotten in over your head," I said. "Are you blackmailing Roger Harper?"

His head snapped up. "How—"

"I just figured it out. I have no evidence, but you're dealing with a dangerous man. Are you blackmailing Gage?"

He shook his head.

"But you tried. Gage knows things have gone wrong and the mother of both of you is dead. I bet he's trying to find Roger because he thinks Roger killed her. I bet he's right."

He nodded. "Do the police think that?"

"Well, they don't have the evidence…that's why they want to find Roger. Do you think he killed her?"

"That bastard won't stop, Gage says."

"So anybody who knows he's not the real Buster is in danger. Fred, you need to run. Go rent a car from Smokey and get the hell out of here."

"But what about—"

"The hell with any of that. Save your skin. Come back when it's over."

He stared at me then rose. "You'll call the cops on me."

"You aren't a priority. They want to keep anyone else from getting killed," I stood. "I'll give you till noon. Either run or turn yourself in to the police. Jail is the safest place for you. I'm serious."

He walked stiffly to the door then he drove away in a silver Camry. I checked the time. Damn. I grabbed a file off my desk and headed toward our temporary conference room in the basement. A contentious divorce meeting awaited me.

By the time I emerged, it was lunch time. I walked across the lobby to my mom's desk.

"I don't really feel like going over to Custer's for the day's inquisition," I said.

"Me neither," she said.

I resolved the matter by buying Joy's lunch if she would bring back lunch for Mom and me. At one o'clock, I called Rachel to tell her about my meeting with Fred.

By three-thirty, I was too antsy to focus on anything at work. With my last appointment finished, I headed home. A State Patrol cruiser was parked in the driveway. Rachel sat at the kitchen table working on her laptop, while Patty watched *Ben-Hur* in the family room.

"I'm supposed to tell Rachel when the chariot race comes on. Then I need to do some vacuuming."

"Well, I'm going to change," I said.

I trudged up the creaky back stairs to find Rachel waiting for me at the top of the front stairwell. She motioned to me. I followed her down the front steps.

"I didn't want to talk in front of Patty," said Rachel. "But there's been three stolen cars reported in the area. I faxed that list Kayla made to Smokey. He said that white Ford Crown Victoria resembled one stolen from his lot. So someone may have been scoping this house yesterday. Oh, and Fred did rent a car from Smokey. So he's probably gone."

"Maybe he won't come back with all the trouble he's in," I said. "At least he won't add to the body count."

At four, I was out in the cold of my backyard in the waning daylight with Merritt, Derek, Kenny, Ryan, and Noah. We practiced shooting our rifles. Merritt passed out cards for a website where we could order safety locks for our guns. A few minutes later, Paul Ritter showed up.

"This is an old hunting rifle my dad gave me," said Paul. "I've never even used it and it must be really old. Would you take a look at it, Officer Merritt, and tell me if it's safe? If it is, I'll get it registered."

While Merritt inspected the rifle, Jay walked out to our group.

"So are you a good shot?" Jay asked me.

"Well, Bill showed me how to use a rifle a few years ago, but no, not really. I'm better with a handgun because that's what I've practiced with at the shooting range."

"Which I hear is doing great business since the double murder," said Jay. "And they've extended their hours since Granny Goblet's death."

"Figures," I said. "Bloody cold out here. Noah and Ryan are the smart ones. They keep running up the hill to set up the cans...so they're warm. Hey, I know Patty doesn't want to impose, but I bet she'd like some things from her apartment."

"Well, you're not going alone."

"I knew you wouldn't want me to. As soon as the group goes inside, you and I could run out there quick and be back for supper."

I didn't know why, but going there seemed critical.

"Are you inviting me for supper?" he asked.

"Sure. Patty's nervous, so she's been cooking up a storm. She's got a vat of stew going…she uses sirloin for stew meat so it's really good."

"Oh, I don't know…I could just hit a greasy fast food place," he said with a smirk then looked over at the guys. "Looks like they're going in."

We walked back to the house with them then I convinced Patty to give me a list of her things. Jay drove me in his cruiser over to Patty's apartment, the lower level of a house on Hickory Avenue. It was strange, but my guts began to churn. Jay unlocked the outside door and we stepped inside to the small foyer. A flight of stairs to the right led to the upper apartment, currently occupied by an elderly deaf man, a cousin of Eldon Strumple.

Suddenly, my heart began to bash against all the other organs in my body. What?

Acting on impulse, I barked, "No!" Then I slapped Jay's hand away from the doorknob and pushed him hard onto the stairs.

Gunshots blasted through the door and into the outer door.

"Shit!" I said and I meant it.

As we pulled our guns, Jay looked at me.

"How did you know—never mind."

When he tried to rise, I lunged across his chest.

"No! Please call for backup. You don't need to play hero for me. Just call."

"Okay, but you need to get behind me."

He slid me off of him then he made the call, reporting his location.

"He's had time to run," said Jay. He crawled on the floor to the other side of the door and finished unlocking it. "Ready?"

I nodded, my gun ready in my sweaty hands, my finger on the Glock safety lever and trigger.

"Police!" he yelled.

When Jay pushed the door open, a gust of cold wind filled the foyer. Jay moved forward, swinging his big-ass gun to the left then the right then back again. I followed him, pointing my gun wherever he wasn't, though I moved in a crouch, scared as I was. When Jay came to the hall, he quickly whipped his body and gun down the hallway, as agile as a tiger, no, a lion in his brown trooper uniform. He motioned me against the living room wall. I crept to the wall, thinking as he did that the thug had fled out the kitchen back door. Jay sprang to the opening of the kitchen. If my heart wasn't pounding so hard, I'd be impressed by him. He looked down on the kitchen floor then peered out of the side of the back door into the darkness.

"Jay, no! Don't go out there, please. He's just waiting to shoot whoever goes out there. Please wait. Please, babe."

"Well, since you called me 'babe.' Would you check him? But stay down."

Creeping into the kitchen, I saw the body of a man in a dark parka, lying face down. The edge of the pooling blood extended beyond the side of his coat.

"Jay, help me turn him over."

Together we turned him over onto his back.

Chapter 20

JAY pressed his fingers against Fred Goblet's neck. "He's still alive."

Fred sputtered. I grabbed dish towels out of the drawer as Jay unzipped the coat and yanked his shirt open.

"One clean hole," Jay said. "Though the back of his head is bloody. Maybe he got ambushed. No gun."

I pressed the towels against the wound, but the blood just kept coming out, more and more and I needed to stop it, but it made my head spin and my stomach swirl and it kept coming. Oh, God. Is he going to die right in front of me?

Jay got back on the phone and requested an ambulance as he kept glancing back at the kitchen door. Then he began to direct the search. I overheard him tell Merritt to stay at Fort Docket.

"Deputy Bo here!" shouted the Dexter second shift officer from the front room.

"Jay Young, State Patrol. Come on back!"

For the first time in my life, I witnessed Bo with his gun drawn. His specialty was calming down drunks, not shooting them.

"Lordy, he looks bad," said Bo. "Just one bullet hole?"

"I think so," I said.

"Put your finger in the hole to stop the bleeding," said Bo.

I stood, squirted my hands with hand soup, and then kneeled back down by Fred. I slowly pressed my index finger into the hole. It made the tile floor swim, so I kept my head down and focused on Fred's face. He sputtered again then opened his eyes.

"I-I shoulda run," he said, wincing. "I followed Roger here. He clobbered me over the head and took my gun. He asked me where Gage was. When I said I didn't know, he shot me."

"Okay, don't talk, just breathe," I said. "No, stay with me, Fred. That's right. Help will be here soon. Just breathe slow."

"Deputy, go search the other rooms," said Jay from his backdoor lookout.

"Right away."

Bo raised his gun as he moved toward the short hallway, with a room on each side and a closet and bathroom at the end of the hall. Compared to the smooth stealth of Jay, Bo was nervous and jerky, but he completed his inspection and returned.

Soon, Sheriff Smythe arrived with a deputy. Paramedics took over and I retreated to the hall bathroom to wash. In the living room, I stared at the flashing red and blue lights. I took out my phone and sent a text to Jay, telling him to write in his report that we jumped out of the way because we heard a sound inside. A few minutes later, he replied.

"I didn't hear anything, did you?" he typed.

"No," I responded.

"Rachel coming to get you. Stay home. I will come when I can."

"Ok."

I took Patty's list from my purse that I'd dumped by the front door. I crept into her bedroom, pulled a suitcase down from the closet then started to fill it. I set the suitcase next to my purse by the front door. Rachel surveyed the scene when she arrived. On our way back to Fort Docket, I gave her my account. At home, I gave Merritt, Jack, and Patty a detailed narrative. Patty called Mom while I tried to eat my stew.

A couple of hours later, Jay arrived. I warmed the stew for him then he talked to Merritt and Rachel about the search for Roger, which had proved unproductive. Fred had been life-flighted to Colorado. Jay ordered Rachel and Merritt to end their shifts and go home, which they agreed to, but stayed for a glass of bourbon. Mom came over for a while to be with Patty. Eventually, Mom, Rachel, and Merritt left, leaving Jack and Patty in the family room watching Young Frankenstein, while Jay and I sat in the living room.

"I inherited this fancy furniture," I said of the room. "I've never really liked it, though I think it's expensive. God above, what a day."

Part of me wanted to collapse, yet the adrenaline still buzzed within me. Jay sat beside me on the sofa, looking intently at me.

"You saved me," he said. "Those shots through the front door would have hit me."

"I felt your danger even though it happened so fast," I said.

Jay leaned in close to me. "What does that mean? Mmmm?" He kissed me. "Am I under your skin?"

More accurately, he'd permeated my bone marrow, but I wasn't ready to say so.

"Then you lunged across me." He pulled me over his chest. "I confess at the time it wasn't sensual, but it is now."

I slid off him. "You're talking too much."

I stood then reached my hand out to him. He took it then he let me tug him up the stairs. Once he shut the door behind us, he scooped me off the floor and kissed me. I liked, no, loved being scooped.

"I've never been rescued. I loved you doing that for me. I'd love to show my appreciation."

"Not just any man could admit that."

He smiled then kissed me. Instead of the bed, he placed me in the arm chair in my sitting area then turned on the gas fireplace. He took the blanket from the loveseat and spread it on the carpet in front of the fireplace. His efficiency made me wonder if he'd thought of this before. He scooped me up again and placed me on the blanket. He kissed me—and I mean every inch of me as he undressed us both. I loved the image of the flame as it danced across his chest. The kissing continued till I thought I'd bust. I reached out for Mr. Majestic, but he caught my hand.

"Babe, you can't even touch me...I'll burst."

He laid me back onto the blanket and whispered in my ear, "I went to the doctor."

"Okay."

"May I...without, you know, a condom? That's big time trust, you know."

"Okay."

As the frigid wind rattled the windows, we heated, moaned, gasped, and exploded. Our love making penetrated deep into the night. As I tried to sleep, he nestled in close to me, with his arm across my back or chest. I'd roll away just so I could turn over, but his body stayed with me, though his eyes never opened. By morning, I was at the edge of my big bed, his warm, hairy arm holding me. When I awoke I realized if he let go, I'd go over the edge. In a blink, I was afraid—would he let me fall away again? His breath warmed my back and my chest swelled and ached.

He awakened with a big goofy smile on his face as he pulled his head out from under my shoulder.

"I can't believe the way you hog the bed," he said.

"Now how was it that I lunged across you? Like this?" I threw myself over his chest, determined to keep things light. "Except you didn't grab my butt then."

"True. I'll handle them both now to make up for my error."

After our shower, we headed down for breakfast. Jack was already gone and Rachel was sitting at the kitchen table eating eggs and toast. She gave me a grin and Patty pinched my arm when Jay walked into the hall to make calls.

"Oh, Merritt called awhile ago," said Rachel. "And it's probably nothing, but Grant has been convicted of DUI, once in Nebraska and once in South Dakota."

I wondered if anyone bothered to tell Gage that Roger was after him.

As soon as I arrived in my office, Roger called.

"Buster, where are you?" I asked. "You said you'd keep in touch."

"I am now. You need to get that money from the insurance company and I mean today."

"That won't be happening. Where are you? Let's talk."

"Then you get that house sold. Do it now or you need to front the money and keep the insurance check. I know Helen needs the money for Mitch."

"You want me to advance the insurance benefit to you? Do you think I'm stupid? Where's your buddy, Gage? Is he hiding like you? Roger, your secret is out."

The line went dead.

I hoped he heard me say the last part. I didn't want him to think I was the only one who knew his real identity.

I rang Jay and told him of the conversation.

"You shouldn't have told him we knew his real identity," said Jay.

"Well, that's where we differ. I want him to run away from here so nobody else dies. You want to catch him. But he's not smart enough to avoid capture." His silence meant he was annoyed at me, so I needed to stroke him. "Hey, you know when we were at Patty's and you were checking for Roger?"

"Yeah."

"You reminded me of a lion...quick, smooth, stealthy, powerful."

"Mmmm. Well, the truth is that I was scared spitless."

"Of course, so was I, but not enough to ignore you."

"So, do I get to come for supper?"

"You're my stud lion, aren't ya?"

He chuckled. "I'll try to get there by six. I'll call if I get held up…and that's possible."

After I hung up the phone, I wondered where Roger was hiding. Maybe I had scared him off. But someone had been helping him to hide. He chased Fred and searched for Gage, so they weren't aiding him. I logged into my secure laptop. Maybe there was something in these files. At least I now had the name of Roger Harper to look for. As I scrolled through the files, I called Jackson Draper, an elder on the Pine Ridge rez. He greeted me then noted I called on my firm's line.

"So, not a social call," he said. "You've had trouble down there."

"And it's not over," I said. "I know the Redmond family originated in your area. Do you know Roger Harper?"

"Yes, I do, but he hasn't been around here in years."

"Good, because if someone in your area is sheltering him, they're in trouble for aiding a murderer."

"This is the problem, Megan. My mother was a Redmond, so I am hesitant to get involved."

"I see."

"So, I want to stay out of the situation and not help you in your search for connections he may have."

"Hmm. Connections, as in say, births or marriages?'

"Yes, that kind."

"I understand. So how have you been? How's your back?"

We chatted for a few minutes then I wished him well. I continued my review of the local Redmond, Goblet, and Percival files. The sky began to darken for the day. Studying the copies of birth certificates and marriage licenses, I noted we didn't have photocopies of all of them, but enough to keep me searching. Then I saw it. Harper.

Shit.

I looked up to find Mom in my doorway.

"I'm heading home," she said. "Everybody else has left."

"Will you be coming for supper?" I asked.

"Yes, Patty said six. She also said you and Jay are back together."

"Who knew we just needed a good life and death scare?"

"I'm glad. Are you leaving soon?"

"In a few minutes."

After she left, I stared at the laptop, wondering about the implications. I logged off then locked my desk and office door. I checked that all office doors had been locked before I headed outside. My mind swirled with the information I'd uncovered. I locked the back door then turned toward my SUV.

The moment I stepped off the curb, a large, meaty hand covered my mouth.

Oh, God! Help me!

Chapter 21

HIS hand was so big it smashed up against my nostrils, blocking my breathing. His other hand was on my shoulder. I plunged my hand into my purse for my gun as I tried to pull away.

Shit! This must be Roger here to kill me.

"Now just settle down," said the voice.

It wasn't Roger.

It was rape.

I swung my right hand back into where I thought his balls would be.

He grunted.

I hit the mark. He let go of me, but I stumbled forward and hit the side of my head on the fender of the Barracuda. I fell to my knees, but now I clutched my Glock as I fell to the side on my hip. I turned enough to aim at the bent over figure as I scrambled back to my knees then to my feet.

The tall man stood with his hands on his knees. It was my chance. I spun the gun around in my hand like Rachel showed me then brought it down hard on his head. He fell forward onto the frozen pavement. I jumped to the side to avoid getting squashed.

I stood panting as I stared at the figure. Dark hair, dirty old wool coat with a body stench that made me step back. I pulled out my phone then paused when he began to stir. Shit. He didn't stay knocked out very long. He looked up at me.

"Oh! No cops! Please!"

Bending down, I placed the barrel of my gun on his forehead.

"You're right—I should just kill you and save the police and the courts the hassle."

"No, please. Roy Jeffries sent me. He said Jackson Draper was asking around about me."

I straightened. "Are you Buster?"

"Yes."

"Darold Redmond?"

"Yes."

"Sit back on the curb," I said as I grabbed a tissue out of my purse for the blood running down the side of my head.

He had a stream of blood running down past his temple and onto his neck. I gave him a tissue.

"Now give me that explanation again."

"I been in prison in Canada. Got out on parole. Worked odd jobs for cash in Canada. Then I went to see some friends on Rosebud, it's a reservation. Pastor Roy Jeffries came and told me about Val. And he told me Jackson Draper was tryin' to find me. Patty White Horse had called him 'while back, said somebody runnin' around sayin' he was me."

"Go on."

"So I went to Pine Ridge and somebody said I should get down here quick. That was yesterday. Said to go see you in private. So that's what I was doin'."

"So why'd you have to attack me? Damn, I nearly shot you."

"I didn't want you to scream."

"I haven't screamed since I was seven, if then. That was a stupid thing to do. Let me see your identification. You can't jump out at people in the dark, especially women, you dumbshit."

"I'm sorry." He handed me his wallet.

"Go back and sit against the wall where the sidewalk is dry…and move slow."

I tried to breathe deeply, but fear had hit me so fast and hard, I felt wobbly as I searched through his wallet. My whatever-you-call-it consistently warned me of impending danger. Why had it failed me tonight? His driver's license appeared legitimate. When I looked closer at him, I noticed a scar running down from his right temple onto his cheek. His skin was lighter than Roger's, and he sported a moustache and goatee on his weather hardened skin.

"Okay, get up," I said. "Can you?"

"Yeah, kinda wobbly. You got me good twice. My pride's hurtin' more than my head."

"Where's your car?"

"On the side street."

"Okay, now. Walk out into the parking lot and come back when I tell you. And you do as I say. I'm a good shot. I've even killed a cop."

"Really?"

"Yeah, DEA. Now walk."

"A'right. Don't know why."

He walked a ways till I told him to stop then he came back.

"You're duck-footed like Val."

"Nothin' to be proud of. Glad Mitch didn't get it."

I studied him and made my plan.

"Okay, I need to make a call. Oh, wait…let's go inside. Stand up against the building."

Shoving my gun up under my arm, I unlocked the door, turned on the light, and punched in my security code. I motioned Buster to the kitchen table then I called Jay.

"I just got here. Where are you?"

"I'm still at the firm. I need to show you something. Would you come here right away?"

"Ah, sure. And you'll explain everything to me. I'm hungry."

"The sooner you come, the sooner you eat."

While we waited, I quizzed Buster on every bit of information he could possibly know about the involved families. He called Fred a "weasel" and Kenny a "hothead."

When Jay arrived five minutes later, my show-and-tell shocked him. As he frisked him, he scolded Buster for scaring me. Jay got out our first aid kit and staunched the bleeding on our heads as he quizzed Buster.

I gave Buster a leftover pastry and a glass of orange juice then I joined Jay in a private consultation on the far side of the room.

"What do we do with him?" Jay asked.

I glanced back at Buster. "He has nine dollars and no credit cards. So feeding him would be a kindness."

When we looked over at him, he looked down as he ate and held paper towels to his head.

"And he needs to be cleaned up. Who's at my house?"

"McNeill will stay till we return and Jack's there with your mom and Bill."

This time when I glanced back at Buster, I knew another reason he'd stayed away from this area. He was always looking at Jay. Guys usually looked at me.

"Did you tell him I'm a cop?"

"No, he's looking at you because he's gay," I whispered.

"Huh? I didn't get that…well, maybe something."

I walked over to Buster. "Did I tell you that my boyfriend here is State Patrol?"

Buster jumped up from his chair, a bite of the pastry falling from his mouth. "No! I didn't mean to hurt her!"

"Buster, you're not in trouble. I'm just telling you so you know he can make things happen. Would you like to see your mom and Mitch?"

"So much I could bust. Like to see Helen's kids, too. Been a long time."

I nodded then walked back over to Jay, who was grinning at me.

"Getting possessive, are we? Don't worry, my electricity only flows one direction. And he's kind of ugly."

"So, we need to do something," I said. "Hey, Patty would know him. She could confirm his identity then we could feed him and get him some decent clothes. And we need to figure out if he needs stitches."

"Okay, let's do that, then we could eat, too."

We walked over to Buster.

"Buster, we're going to take you to Megan's house. We'll give you supper and a shower and get your head bandaged. Okay?"

"Yes, sir. What do I do with my car?"

"It's fine where it is. We'll get it later. But why don't you pull it into the lot and get what you need out of it? Then I'll drive you in my truck to the Docket house."

A few minutes later, Jay pulled up in the driveway behind me. I closed the garage and dashed into the house, now aware I should warn people of our visitor.

"Um, hello," I said to Patty, Mom, Bill, Rachel, and Jack. "We have a guest. I need to let him in."

I went to the front door then escorted Buster into the kitchen.

"Oh, my Lord!" blurted Patty. "Buster!"

Patty went up and hugged him.

"It's good to see you, Patty," said Buster. "I didn't know if anyone would remember me."

"Of course. Hey, have you seen your mom yet? Oh! You're bleeding."

"So is Megan," said Mom.

"What happened?" asked Patty.

"Well, a stranger approached me in the dark," I said. "I overreacted, as in I pistol-whipped him."

"It was my fault," Buster said.

"Let me look at that, Buster," said Rachel. "Sit down." She parted his hair. "Oh, Megan you nailed him. He needs stitches. Let me look at you."

I walked over to her. I didn't need to sit down for her to check my head.

"No, you're okay."

"We don't really want to take Buster to the ER...we need to keep him under wraps," said Jay.

"I can put them in," said Rachel. "I'll get my stuff out of my car. I'll do it in the mud room if it's all right with Buster."

He nodded.

"I think we could both do with some aspirin, bourbon, and supper," I said.

"Finally, the real deal," said Patty. "Still, he needs a shower before I could sit at a table with him," she whispered.

"I think he's pretty much broke," I said. "He's been in Canada, so he didn't get the news about Val till just recently. They told him on the rez to come down here."

"Okay, so he showers and we feed him then what?" asked Jay.

"I could let him sleep on one of the sofas in the basement," I said.

"Now, wait," said Bill. "What was he in prison for?"

"Assault and battery," I said.

"And you're going to let him sleep here?"

"Well, I think he seems pretty even-tempered. I did kick him in the balls and bash him over the head, but he doesn't seem to hold that against me. I don't think he's a danger...to us."

"You don't feel he's dangerous?" asked Patty. "Explain what happened that you both come here bloody."

"I-I didn't have any sense of impending trouble...nothing. So either I've lost that ah, peculiarity, or he's not a danger. Something else, do we really want him on the loose? If he doesn't know now, he'll soon find out his mother is under police protection from his impersonator. That's trouble, but for tomorrow, so let's keep him here now."

"Okay, now who is he?" asked Mom.

"He's Val's brother," I said.

"Are we sure?"

"We'll be taking him to see his mother in the morning—she'll be the ultimate proof," I said.

"And who is Roger Harper?" she asked.

"Well, it is confusing," I said. "Roger would be an illegitimate son of Howard Redmond. So Roger and Buster would be half-brothers, that's why they look alike. Though, now that I've seen them both, I think Roger fooled people mostly because Buster hadn't been around for several years."

Jay left when his phone rang.

"Yeah, there are some differences," said Mom.

"Gage must have known of Roger, so he hired him to play Buster so they could split the insurance money and maybe the estate. But Roger panicked when people began to question his identity...that's why he killed Granny. Gage lost control of his puppet. So now they're enemies. Fred figured it out then blackmailed Roger, which is why Roger shot Fred."

Jay came back into the kitchen. "Well, damn. We've lost track of Gage—he's a sneaky so and so. And we don't know where Roger is. Dave is supposedly at the hospital with Fred. But he might sneak off, too."

"Dave is probably more honest, but maybe he'll try to avenge Fred," I said.

Jay scratched his late day whiskers. "We don't have jurisdiction in Colorado, though I put in a call to the FBI there."

While Buster showered, Patty warmed up supper and Mom tended my cut. After supper, Buster gladly accepted a glass of bourbon. We told him of our plans to keep him here for the night then take him.to his mother's house in Sidney tomorrow.

During the evening, I took Jay and Rachel aside.

"I don't like it that Mitch doesn't have any police on the premises," I said. "Yes, I know Drew is there and the cops stop by, but he's not protected well enough. He's still the one who stands to gain the most from the insurance payouts and the sale of the house."

"I don't have any free officers," said Jay. "My department budget is already drowning in overtime commitments. Oh, and now Dave has disappeared. I've asked the FBI for help…but I don't know if I'll get it."

"How 'bout this," said Rachel. "I'll park my cruiser in the Percival driveway overnight so it looks like a cop is spending the night. I can get a ride back to my apartment. I'll get the cruiser again in the morning on my way here."

"Do you really think the danger is still so great for Mitch or even Patty and Pearl since you told Roger his secret identity was exposed?" asked Jay.

"You did?" asked Rachel.

"Yeah, he tried to talk me into pushing to get the money from the insurance company today. Then I told him we knew who he really was. Then he hung up. So, no, I don't know who's in danger. Maybe Roger and Gage will shoot it out. But something is up. I'm feeling that more clearly by the minute."

"Well, think about this—both Roger and Gage should be really angry with you and your interference," said Jay. "You've kept the insurance companies from paying. They might like to see you die first…before they run or kill each other."

Triple shit.

Chapter 22

A S much as I would've enjoyed seeing mother and son reunited, I told Jay he needed to take Buster to see her so I could make it to an appointment. Actually, it wasn't till later, but I needed to get to the quiet of my office so I could concentrate. Jay reluctantly agreed and even promised to take Buster to buy clothes on the way to Pearl's once Rachel arrived for the day.

At work, I closed my office door, sat at my desk, and got angry. Roger was on the loose and the murders of Junior and Val remained unsolved. At least one matter I could attend to, but I needed to wait till the right time. I reviewed two depositions then promptly at nine-thirty, I left for Sidney. I waved to my mom as I crossed the lobby, but felt her concerned look boring a hole into the side of my head.

I rang the doorbell of the pale gray, two-story. The white door was opened by Helen. I didn't wait for her to invite me in; I pushed past her into the living room. Death upon death, my anger must have shown on my face, for Helen started to speak then stopped.

"Did you know about the scheme to murder Val and Junior for their insurance money?" I asked sharply. "Or should I ask how you helped Roger Harper?"

"I-I didn't know anything until Roger showed up to see us with those Disney videos," she said. "He took me aside and told me he didn't kill anyone, but was just supposed to play Buster so the insurance money would get paid out."

"So you knew Mitch would collect on one policy then Kenny and Mitch would collect on the other. And you wanted to help your ex-husband stay out of trouble because you of all people know what he is like. You planned to help Roger collect money that wasn't his."

"Buster is the criminal. They should've kept him in prison."

"Because of your concealment, Granny Goblet is dead. Then he tried to kill Fred, but he's supposed to pull through. And he told the police who shot him."

"He's a criminal, too," she said.

"You stupid bitch! Without the protection of police and others, Roger might have killed my Patty or Pearl. Don't you get it?"

"I don't care about them!" she snapped.

Then she lunged at me, swinging her open hand at my head. I ducked and punched her in the gut as hard as I could. She crumpled to knees.

"Does your family know you've been hiding a murderer? Do you want them to find out that you've sheltered someone who'd like to see Mitch die?"

She lifted her head. "No! Oh, God! I never meant for that." She began to weep.

I believed her, but marveled at her stupidity. "You dumb hick, how could you not know that? If Roger and Gage had succeeded with their plan, they'd get more money if Mitch died."

Helen rolled over onto the carpet, face down, and wept into her hands.

"Mitch still isn't safe," I said. "Do you understand that?"

I took a photocopy of her marriage license and set it by her head. She grabbed it and tore it up. I put another one on the other side of her head. She looked at it and wailed.

"The petition for the guardianship and conservatorship was rejected because Kenny was still a suspect in the double murder. But you're the guilty one."

"What are you going to do to me? Do the police know?" she asked as she sat up.

"No, but they'll figure it out. The FBI is now involved."

"Oh, God! I didn't understand. Please believe me."

"Actually, I do. And your stupidity might just save you. I'll get Rich on your case. You see, I don't care a bit about you, but I do care about Mitch, so you have an ally in me…one who will try to keep you home taking care of that boy. But I'll make sure you never control his money."

"But my family will hate me."

"Okay, for now, they don't need to know. I'm not even going to tell the police. If they come to talk to you, keep your silence and tell them Rich is your attorney."

"Not you?"

"No, Rich knows the criminal side of things. I'll stay with the money side." I paused. "No, go ahead and tell them I'm your attorney. That might send them to me before they arrest you. Just don't say anything to anyone. And don't talk to Roger. Call the police if he comes here."

I left her on the floor. On the other side of the street was Mom's Nissan. I walked over to her as she rolled down her window.

"No way was I letting you go anywhere alone," said my mom. "Jay told me you were more in danger than Patty now."

A black Camry stopped behind Mom's car. When the car door opened, I located my Glock in my purse. A tall man with dark hair stepped into the street.

"Easy, hon. Jay called Robert Foxworthy and said you were in danger," said Mom.

Tony approached. He'd spent time undercover as a cowboy for Bill when the area suffered from problems with meth trafficking. He'd been convincing as a cowhand—he looked like the Marlboro Man. In time, he'd caught the eye of Vonny, Derek's sister.

"I understand you're causing more trouble," said Tony.

"As always," Mom said.

I shrugged then asked, "Did you bring Vonny?"

"Yeah, she took a couple of days off. What were you doing here?"

"Talking to Helen...making sure she understands the danger Mitch is in," I said. "Well, thanks for your concern, but I'm going back to work."

Back in my office, I called Werner Electric. A female voice answered. After I identified myself, I asked for Gage, but was told he wasn't there. I asked for Grant, who answered.

"What do you want?" Grant said. "My brother—"

"Is going to be dead if he doesn't go to the police," I said. "Roger is after him."

"Who's Roger?"

"The phony Buster your brother hired."

"Huh?"

"They were in a deadly scheme together and it went wrong. Roger tried to kill Fred Goblet last night."

"What the hell? What's goin' on?"

What a dolt—no wonder Gage didn't want his brother's help.

"Just tell Gage to turn himself in to the police. It's the safest place for him."

"Dammit! What's goin' on? Fred got shot burglarizing an apartment."

"Grant, was Gage really at the shop all afternoon on the day Junior and Val were killed?"

The line went dead. Well, at least I tried to warn Gage, though he probably understood the danger. Now maybe Grant did. How it would help, I didn't know.

Appointments and deadlines forced me to keep my mind on work till after four when I left for home, restless and apprehensive. Rachel was reading my Edgar Allan Poe anthology in the family room. I went up to change. I wished I could relax well enough to read, but it didn't seem likely. I said things would happen fast; they had and would continue that way. I put on some jeans and a navy sweater. I went down the back stairs, the creaking wooden steps echoing against the walls of the narrow, closet-like room. I thought about Junior's house. Those wood floor planks probably creaked.

Creaking wood. Surprise. Two innocent people stone dead. Wood floors. Poe. Wood.

I dashed back to grab my purse, then ran back down the stairs. Rachel looked up from her book just before I yanked it out of her hand. The table of contents. I heard my own heart pounding now. Page 445—I found it. Junior gasping in surprise as Death approached. Hearts pounding, victims and killer alike. Louder and louder. Would the sound be heard by a neighbor? She screamed. Done so quickly, planned so well. We found the tell-tale hearts—where was the killer?

"Come with me," I said to Rachel.

"But I need to stay here," she said.

I put on my coat and headed for the garage door.

"Where are you going?" asked Patty.

"We need to solve two murders. Call Derek to come over."

In a flash, I was in the Barracuda. Rachel followed in her cruiser. She was on the phone most of the way.

I parked in front of the Percival house. The sky was beginning to darken, the eerie slashes of red and orange across the horizon unnerved me. My hands shook as I hastened to unlock the front door. Inside, I stopped to hear the gasp of surprise and the grunt. The stain of blood was still on the floor boards. I walked into the kitchen where Val had lain. The plan wasn't to conceal the deaths; it was to conceal the killer. Wooden something. No trace of an escape. So clever.

Rachel came up behind me, but I ignored her. I'd felt his presence. Where? In the new addition. The glass doors were no longer chained shut. I opened them. Lew and Hank were nearly done. The walls and ceiling were finished. The carpet and padding were cut and laid out with the roll of carpet stopping ten feet from the west wall where the plywood box remained. Once the fireplace was installed, the carpet would be stapled down and the baseboards installed—it would be complete.

I turned to Rachel who looked annoyed.

"Help me find a screwdriver or a hammer," I said.

"Why?"

I walked around, but Hank and Lew had removed all their tools.

"Do you have a crowbar in your cruiser?" I asked.

"Yeah, but I want to know why you need it."

My guts began to roil. Where was my purse?

"If you get it, I'll show you where Gage Redmond hid while the police searched the scene."

"You know?" She looked around. "Where?"

I stared at her.

"Fine," she said as she turned around.

I followed her into the front room where I left my purse. As it was now dark, she flipped on the porch light. As soon as she stepped onto the porch, an arm came down and she fell. When he stepped into the light, he looked down at Rachel then at me.

Chapter 23

ROGER took a step forward then turned sharply to his left, raised his gun and fired. In that instant, I moved—dashing into Mitch's bedroom. I locked the door and ran through the door that led to the master bedroom. I closed the door behind me. I heard Roger trying to bust down Mitch's door.

Oh, God! Help me, sweet Jesus, or I'm dead.

I ran through the master bedroom into the laundry-bathroom, leaving that door open. I needed to get behind him somehow—I sure didn't want a face-to-face shootout. As I ran into the TV room, doors crashed against walls behind me. Then I knew where to go. I waited till I was sure he was running through the laundry room then I turned back to the kitchen. I'd cleaned the food out of the house a couple of weeks ago, so the cupboards were empty. I opened the tall cabinet, a small pantry of sorts, and scooted in. The middle shelf was lacking a support so I had set that shelf on top of the shelf above. That gave me and other people my size, third graders, room to squeeze in. I stuck my left thumb in the bottom of the door so that I had a millimeter or so to peek out.

From my location, I could hear Roger stumble against the stacked washer and dryer. He spewed profanities. The door leading into the TV room smashed against the DVD shelf. My heart pounded so hard I thought it would burst through my chest. My breathing became faster and shallower as I heard quick, dull thuds—it was my own heart. The pounding grew louder as I tried to hear Roger. The throbbing moved into my ears, I could no longer hear anything except the incessant hammering of my heart, inside the wood. Louder. Louder. I wanted to scream—the fear made me gasp for air. He would hear the pounding!

A figure in a dull gray coat moved into view, his heels toward me.

Now!

I pushed the door open. He whirled around to feel the bullets rip into his chest. As my shots entered him, his blood spurted out. His gun fired as he fell backward. I kept firing until he fell against the sink and onto the floor. His head slammed against the floor. Rising from my crouch, I stepped to his side and I looked down at his dark eyes, now empty of life and his evil spirit. I turned away then took a deep breath.

Nevermore, you bastard.

Silence. Two moments.

Then footsteps in the room behind me then into the TV room. He'd been followed! God above, who was this? They didn't call my name or his name. I flattened myself against the wall next to the roll-top desk.

Gage walked into the room, looked down at Roger, and then raised his gun toward the front room where he thought the shots came from. Then he took another step. Now I was behind his right shoulder, a body-length away. As I lifted my gun, I wrapped my left hand around the bottom of the Glock.

"Stop!" I yelled.

He did.

"Gage, you make a choice. Put down your gun or I'll shoot you through the skull. Look down at what I can do. Roger chose wrong."

Roger lay on his back; the front of his coat was shredded in a line of holes and blood. The first shots hadn't killed him so the blood poured out of him till my last bullets hit his neck and head.

"Why kill me?" he asked.

"Because you murdered Junior and Val."

"Oh, how'd I do that?"

"Drop your gun, you cocky son of a bitch."

"I'd like to hear how I could have possibly killed them. I was at my shop. I had witnesses."

"You drugged your brother. What was it? Some potent sleeping pills you put in his coffee? He slept through your murders, while you were here. You got one of Kenny's rifles then approached Junior with a question about it. Then you shot him through the head. They trusted you and you knew so much about their routine, right down to the minute. Then you turned on the TV real loud and chased Val into the kitchen. You bashed her head against the door then blasted her."

"Interesting. How do you know all this?"

"I heard them…they told me."

"What? Where were you?"

"In my office."

"I've heard about you. You're crazy."

"Then so no one could see you or track you, you hid in the fireplace enclosure in the new room. Then it would look like only Kenny was here if the cops saw past your phony murder-suicide set-up."

"Oh, now isn't that all so clever. How did I then escape?"

"You walked out the back door of the new additions, to which you had a key, locked it, and then climbed that ladder onto those thick tree limbs. It was just enough to keep you from making tracks in the snow. Then you climbed over the fence to the Strumple yard then over it into the alleyway where you could escape."

"Oh, and I bet you're just so proud of yourself, figuring this all out."

"Proud? No, angry, so angry that I want you to make a move. I want to blast your brains out that window. My God, what an evil piece of shit. Val was a mother and your half-sister! You killed your own blood for fifteen or twenty grand or whatever your cut was. Or did you plan on killing Roger so you'd get the whole twenty-five grand? Was

Mitch next? Your mother died because of you. So turn around! Do it!"

"I'm not going to prison."

"Then let me send you to hell."

He turned his head just a smidgen then booming shots rang out from the TV room and Gage fell forward.

I gasped then swung my gun to the north doorway.

"It's me, babe!"

"Oh, Jay!" I looked down at Gage's still form as I dropped my gun to the linoleum. "God Almighty!"

Merritt came in the front door, Loske came in behind Jay. And Tony came through the master bedroom door. I hadn't heard them—I was so focused on Gage. Merritt and Loske checked the men.

"You had Gage scared all right," said Loske. "Look on the floor at that puddle. He pissed his pants."

"Big man," Jay said. "He could kill defenseless people, but he couldn't handle—what does Beulah call you? 'Shrimpy girl.' That's it."

"How's Rachel?" I asked as I pressed my hands against my sides so no one could see them shaking.

"She's conscious now...Roger pistol-whipped her, good and hard," said Merritt. "She'll have a nasty concussion."

Outside a siren blared as it came to a stop.

"She called us on the way here," said Jay. "I knew it was trouble. Turns out you didn't really need us."

"Oh, I was ready to blast Gage, but I'm glad I didn't need to."

"By the way, we found Dave," said Merritt. "He was in pursuit, too. But when Roger then Gage ran in the house, he stopped to help Rachel."

"Finally, one decent human in all of this. Who did Roger shoot at?" I asked.

"Gage, I think," said Merritt. "Gage followed anyway. Then Dave dragged Rachel away from the front door so they wouldn't get hit by the bullets he thought would go flying."

"So, did Roger follow me here?" I asked.

"Probably," said Tony. "He kept stealing and dumping cars, but in a dinky town, you can only hide so well. I was a couple of blocks behind him. And get this—the last car he stole came from the parking lot of Docket Law." He chuckled. "He hot-wired the car belonging to the real Darold H. Redmond."

Jay smiled. "And probably never knew it."

"So why did you come here?" asked Merritt.

"I thought maybe I figured out his hiding place after the murders, but I needed to see it again."

"How was it you surprised Roger?" asked Merritt.

"I hid."

Everyone looked around.

"Where?" asked Jay.

I opened the pantry door.

I walked away from their chortling into the north addition.

"I feel responsible," I said. "I sent Rachel out to get a crowbar. That's when Roger got her. But now that I think about it, I bet—"

I walked up to the plywood enclosure then pulled back on the top edge. It came easily. Jay stepped forward and held one side as we peered into the opening for the fireplace.

"See, these nail heads are fake," I said. "Look, Gage even pounded in chunks of wood he could hold onto while he was in there. Lew built this out far enough for a fireplace...so even a tall man could sit easily in there. Then the snake slithered out when it was dark and after the police shut the door to this cold room. Until then, Gage sat and listened to the deputies run around."

"That's why you said you felt danger when you came into this room—Gage, the killer, was still here," said Jay.

"Then he made his escape out back and returned to the shop to rouse Grant."

"Grant was sure Gage was in the shop all afternoon," said Merritt.

"But when he awakened, he was embarrassed he'd slept so late. He probably couldn't figure out why he was knocked out so long, though by now he may have guessed that his brother drugged him. He has a DUI, right? So he's not keen on letting people think he's a drunk who slept through the late afternoon at work. And he wanted to protect his brother, but he didn't understand what he'd done. So he lied that he saw Gage."

"How did Roger stay hidden from us?" asked Merritt.

I busied myself looking into the fireplace. When I turned around, I said, "I'm never going to sell this place. Four deaths. That'll scare everyone away."

Jay nodded, but kept his eyes on me.

"Can I get some air?" I asked. "And I'd like to go see Rachel. I dragged her into this mess today."

"We need to surrender our guns," said Jay who looked to Tony.

"Sure, I can take them," he said. "And you'll need to give statements."

Jay escorted me past the bloody bodies and out into the welcome cold air of the porch. I looked back and nobody was following closely.

"I'll say Gage started to move his gun toward me," I said.

Jay said nothing, he just looked at me.

"He'd only moved his head, but he deserved to die," I said.

"I wasn't going to risk him shooting you."

"Right, he started to move his gun toward me. I'll say those exact words. And he said he wasn't going to prison. There was only one option for him. You just beat him by a nanosecond."

The door opened behind us.

"Are you ready for the statements?" asked Tony.

I looked out at the neighbors standing on the sidewalk, with Chief Tate and Deputy Bo holding them back.

"God above, I don't want to go back in there," I said.

"We could go into one of the bedrooms," suggested Tony.

I turned to Jay. "Will you call and check over at Mitch's…to make sure everything is okay?"

"I will while you give your statement. Megan, just focus on that. I'll wait in the kitchen."

When I finished talking to Tony, I flicked off the outside light then stepped onto the porch. It was bloody cold, but out of the north wind. Soon Jay came out.

"I'm done in there," I said. "The blood makes it smell like a slaughterhouse. There's a lot of it."

"You know we did what we had to do."

I nodded.

"Oh, I called home and told them you were fine. And everything is okay at Mitch's. I do need to stay for a while."

"Okay, uh, will you get my purse? I can't think now where it is. Then I'm going to see Rachel."

After my visit to a groggy Rachel, I headed home then went where I needed to go. Nobody protested—they knew better. I put on snow boots, pants, and my heaviest coat then walked past Mom, Bill, Patty, and all the other faces there. I did pause to hug Vonny, but I didn't say anything. I trudged through the three or four inches of crusty snow, blown into hardened icy waves across the yard and over the buffalo grass. I walked beyond the area lit by the back porch light into the darkness. The quarter moon showed the huge mass of snow drifted against the west side of Rufus. I climbed the low hill; the wind slapped at my face till I reached the top and could turn to the east. As a kid, I'd played here with Derek and Vonny. Then the Four Bastards set a cross afire last fall. But I'd reclaimed it as the Docket representative and as the only one crazy enough to care about a grassy mound in the family wasteland.

I killed a man tonight.

How could I be a person who could calm volatile family members in the midst of divorce or death and love as hard and as passionately as I did, and yet be able to tear open a man with my slimline subcompact automatic 9mm pistol? Oh, and was also the one who heard the soothing voices of deceased friends and the screams of terror from people nearing death and the wails of a twin beyond my memory.

Roger deserved to die—it was him or me—and I obliged him. But by God's mercy, I lived. Again. God, why did you give me such mercy? You let me live. You gave me the gift of what would you call it? Gumption? I didn't freeze in a crisis, which enabled me to shoot down my attackers. It was an unusual gift. God, you filled my basket with strange gifts; and good ones, too. I nearly missed out on securing Jay. He was strange, too. I could tell by the way he looked at me that he was impressed by my ability to act and think and by my peculiarities.

But God, I did right today, didn't I? This wasn't the time to turn the other cheek. Roger would just kill more people. If he killed me then he'd continue firing at Gage and Jay and Tony and Merritt and anybody else. He was so anxious to get to me that he didn't bother killing Rachel. She got off with a concussion and several stitches, but she'd live. Thank you, God that only two bad guys died today and Patty and Mitch and Pearl were safe. So, didn't I do right? Sweet Jesus, Lamb of God, please intercede for me. I need your forgiveness, Lord. I was so scared and angry that maybe I didn't try hard enough to persuade Gage to surrender. I figured out how he killed Junior and Val and I accused him and gloated. That was wrong of me. So, God, please forgive me for my pride and my fear and my anger and my surging adrenaline that I didn't contain.

I lifted my head to the sky, speckled with stars in the ink, and then lost my balance in the wind and dropped to my knees. I just stayed that way, it wasn't cold through my snow pants and nearly all the snow had been blown off the hill days ago. Surrounded by white ground, weird rocky formations, and a dark blue sky, I still saw blood—on their bodies, on the linoleum, splattered on the cabinet, the old darkened stain on the wood floor. God, you kept me alive when so much evil existed. The hot gun in my hand that didn't shake until I ceased firing. God, please help me be a good Christian daughter, niece, neighbor, attorney, friend, girlfriend. Please don't let me be evil. Open, empty eyes. Holy Spirit comfort me, you know I need it, even when the bad guy comes to kill me and my finger presses the trigger and the blood spurts out and makes puddles on the floor. Good Shepherd, lead me—I'm lost without you. Did I go astray? Did I? God, please protect Mitch and help me figure out what to do with Helen. Mitch is better off with her. If Helen goes to jail, Celeste doesn't go to college; instead, she stays home to care for him and never gets the chance to prove her father wrong. God, help that family. Help me help them.

I rose to my feet. I was alive. Please, God, never let me take that for granted.

Chapter 24

BACK inside, I shook off the snow, took off my coat and boots, and then went into the family room where my gang waited for me. After I ate the truffles Patty gave me, I narrated the events of the evening. Then we ate ham and a green bean concoction and later root beer floats. By the time Jay arrived at ten, I'd already finished one brandy. Jay caught up with me in consumption then put away his brandy in record time.

He caught me alone in the kitchen. "On the way here, I drove to your church. It was locked so I just sat on the front steps to pray. Look, ah, I know you wouldn't be a frisky...frankly, neither am I...but can I stay? I killed a man today and I don't want to be alone."

I smiled, kissed him, and then said, "Yeah. I did my praying out on Rufus. It seemed natural to risk freezing my face to talk to God. And it's the one place I know I can be alone."

Deep in the night, Jay was the first to awaken with a nightmare. He sat up, huffing hard. "I dreamt I was too slow." He took off his shirt and wiped the sweat from his face.

Later it was my turn. Shaking, I said, "I was full of holes and drowning in my own blood."

I turned on the fireplace then crawled back into bed. We drifted back to sleep, with the fire, even a gas one, helping to chase away the terrible thoughts and memories that come so easily in the dark. Several more nightmares shocked us awake and shook our shivering, sweaty bodies. As the first glimmer of light began to lighten the eastern sky, I scooted in close to him. How did I exist those weeks without him?

I took the next day off—one should always do that after one has survived a gunfight. It just seemed right. Jay started paid administrative desk duty that morning. I drove to Sidney and brought Rachel home to convalesce. I received calls from Jackson and Robert Foxworthy. Meanwhile, Vonny spent the day with me, Patty, and Rachel, who lapsed into sleep often.

Just before ten, Melanie called to warn me that Dave Goblet came to the firm looking for me. I asked her to call Chief Tate. I realized I didn't have a gun. Vonny ran over and got their shotgun, with Derek in pursuit.

The moment Dave stepped onto our porch, Tate was behind him and Derek was at the front door with the shotgun. Despite the cold, Tate made Dave take off his coat then he frisked him.

Dave cooperated then saw me behind Derek. "I just want to talk to you."

"Let him come in," I said. "I wasn't in the mood to work today."

Dave nodded as he stepped into the foyer, shivering. He looked around. "Wow, this is gorgeous." He took a few steps toward the living room. "This is high-end American Colonial."

"I inherited it, "I said. "The chairs aren't comfortable with their stiff backs and minimal padding."

"No, it's meant to be looked at. Tell me if you ever plan to sell it. These antiques appreciate with time and these are pristine."

"I never sit here," I said as I sat down on the sofa and let my legs dangle in the air. "See?"

"Yeah, my daughters have the same problem." He gazed at me. "I talked to Fred. He knows you helped to save his life."

"I need to work on my first aid skills. Deputy Bo told me what to do."

"But you did it and Fred would be dead if you and that cop hadn't come when you did."

"That was just luck. Patty, do we have any coffee on?"

"Sure do. I'll meet you in the family room."

Once there, Dave looked out the back windows. "Is that where they burned the cross?"

I nodded. "That's Rufus."

"Yeah, right. Glad you caught them. I heard they'll get prison terms."

Patty brought back a tray of cups and a coffee pot. She poured the coffee and let us prepare our brew as we wished.

"I just wanted to come and tell you that you have no enemies among the Goblets. Abby and Gabby are mad at Fred, or will be whenever he can come home. His deceit will bust our agency."

"You'll be all right," I said. "You showed your smarts last night when you didn't come charging into the house. Roger was ready to shoot anybody."

"How is Officer McNeill?"

"She's upstairs sleeping," I said. "She'll be okay in time."

He nodded.

"I was thinking I would churn out another edition of the Dexter Gazette. I suppose people will want to know what happened."

"Send copies to Kimball."

"Will do."

Dave left after a bit of small talk. I thanked Tate and Derek then helped Patty clear the coffee things. We ignored the reporters who came to the door and called on the phone.

I spent the next hour working on the Dexter Gazette. I let Patty proofread it then she read it to Rachel. I called Merritt, after I determined Jay would be in an extended meeting, to make sure I wasn't charged with any crime and to ask his opinion of my latest edition of the misadventures of Megan Docket. With his blessings, I faxed copies to a couple of diners in Kimball and another three in Sidney.

Then I emailed copies to Brian and Zane, and then to my aunts and uncles in Omaha. We printed out a stack and Patty made deliveries to Custer's and Shaver's, the grocery store.

The house was full that evening. After supper, Jay took my hand and led me down the hall to the living room to talk, but there were still people in the dining room. We paused when we heard Lew exclaim once again his shock that Gage had hidden in the fireplace enclosure. We then backtracked to the study.

"I've had the most brilliant idea," he said. "I think we should get married."

I gasped.

"I know it's a shock—I've never seen your face turn that color of green before. But think about it. We've killed people, we live dangerous lives—we're ruined for anyone normal. You found that out with Brian. My dad and Alison, my old girlfriend, both thought I should go into politics. But that repulses me."

"Me, too," I managed to say when I started breathing again.

"And I love you and I want to grow old with you and we can watch each other's skin shrivel and our hair go gray."

I just blinked.

"Now, I think I know you well enough that this is going to make your head whirl. So I don't have a ring for you because you'll need to mull this over. So please don't answer or even say it's too soon. It doesn't need to be soon. Just someday or some year." He took my hand. "Now before you say anything, 'cause I'm not sure you're even breathing, let's go have some brandy and celebrate the fact we're alive."

I blinked some more then he led me into the kitchen.

Just before we joined that group, he whispered in my ear, "I bought some new underwear—just for your eyes."

That kicked my heart back into rhythm.

"Mmm-mm. Are you wearing them?" I asked, running my hand up the side of his leg.

"No, I was worried about…containment. Good thing, now stop touching me."

"I can't wait for all these people to go away."

Before they did, I sat with Rachel for a few minutes in the family room.

"We all heard that the Redmonds resented the Goblets because Lucy left Howard and the four boys," I said. "But what if that was wrong or maybe the resentment also extended to Howard's new family, which seems to have been more peaceful? Maybe Gage hated his father for remarrying into a better home."

"And hated Pearl, Val, and Buster by extension," said Rachel.

"We heard about the feud between the families and decided it was wimpy…but then five deaths occur."

"Well, hopefully, it's over. Dave made his peace. Hey, when do you think you'll put the Percival house on the market?" asked Rachel.

"Well, Lew and Hank need to finish and I've got a company coming out to replace the blood-soaked slats in the front room then get it all refinished—that's covered by insurance—and not a policy sold by Fred Goblet. So a couple of weeks at a minimum. Then there are two new pools of blood on the kitchen linoleum. Why, know of a buyer?"

"Yeah, me."

"Really?"

"I like that house. I might want to upgrade that fireplace, put in some bookshelves alongside it, kind of like you have, just on a smaller scale."

"I guess the killings wouldn't bother you."

"No, see, there was also justice in that house. I just wish I'd been conscious to see it or to help. Who knew Edgar Allen Poe would help you solve a murder?"

Finally, the house cleared out and Rachel went to bed in the guest room.

"C'mon, Leo," I said.

"What? Who's Leo?" asked Jay.

"It's Latin for lion. Do you have them?"

"I'll get 'em out of my coat and meet you up there."

Royal blue with white pinstripes. Contour maps aren't this entertaining in school. He scared me into heart palpitations with his talk of marriage, but he was fun. Later we cuddled together, staring at the fireplace.

"So, while you're thinking about marrying me or running away with a shriek, I think we should go on vacation," he said.

"Vacation? What's that?"

"Two weeks."

"Two whole weeks?"

"In Europe."

"Wow, you dream big," I said. "I've always wanted to go back."

"Where would you want to go?"

"Oh, anywhere really."

"I was thinking a stop in New York City would be cool...I've always wanted to go there. Then how about London, Berlin, and Paris in May?"

He was hitting all the right buttons—sexy underwear and Europe.

Chapter 25

AFTER breakfast, Jay left for home and the gym, where he'd be the mega-stud, the guy who gunned down a murderer and saved his girlfriend. While he was basking in the macho glow, I'd be heading to Sidney to take Pearl and Buster to see Mitch and his new family. But I still needed to figure out how to handle Mitch's finances. Then an idea struck me. I invited Mom to come with me. She'd met Buster and was willing to meet Pearl, but then she started chatting about all the reading she'd done on autistics.

"Did you know they still don't know what causes autism?" she said. "It sure isn't vaccines. Scientists think it's probably a combination of factors that may differ from one person to the next. Oh, and I baked a pan of brownies for Buster and Pearl, and another pan for Mitch to share."

We both chuckled at her last remark because Mitch only understood his own needs. Celeste told me once that what's his is his, what's yours is his. Ryan told me he was a food thief that could swipe a piece of toast off your plate faster than you could blink.

Pearl lived in a white two-story with green shudders and a screened front porch. As Mom and I climbed the porch steps, we passed dormant brown shrubs that would burst with yellow Mums in the warm weather.

We both recalled our social call to Ellie Bolger's house last summer for Mom said, "This doesn't look like the House of Usher."

"No, this will be very different," I said. "Did you know I'm the agent on her living will? She decided that before we'd even met."

"Word gets around."

Within a few minutes, Mom and I were seated on a sofa in Pearl's living room drinking tea with honey. Pearl and Buster sat in chairs opposite us. The room was clean and warm, though the furniture was showing its age.

"It's so good to have my Buster around again," said Pearl. "Been fixin' some things around here. That's so nice. Oh, and I heard about your derring-do at the Percival house. Glad you're okay."

"It was scary, I'll admit that," I said. "And I'm so glad you stayed out of it, Buster."

"Oh, I was ready, but Mom settled me down, said let the professionals handle it," he said then chuckled. "But you're supposed to be an amateur. Guess they know better. Mom showed me all the copies of the Dexter Gazette you've sent out. I grew up hearin' about the Quinn murders."

"So what are you planning, Buster?" I asked.

"Don't rightly know. I need somethin' and soon...I'm eating up all my Mom's food. Too old for cowhand work. I can do odd jobs. Like workin' by myself...don't always want to be around too many people. Well, never do. And it's hard to get respectable work with my prison record."

"Have you ever considered driving a truck?" I asked.

"Yeah, sure have, but can't pay for the training."

"Well then, you probably qualify for the Docket scholarship fund. Most good jobs require training."

"A scholarship?"

"Yes. We're providing funds for college and vocational training. Just don't tell people, we can only help a limited number. How's your driving record?"

"It's fine. That's not the record I'm worried about."

"With the right references, you'll be fine. We'll talk about it later. Shall we go see Mitch?"

A few minutes later, we pulled into the Percival driveway. Kenny opened the door. Buster greeted him with a
handshake and a shoulder pat. He greeted Helen, Ryan,
Noah, and Celeste, who all stayed back until they saw me
and my mom. After the greetings were over, there was a
moment of awkward silence that needed to be broken.

"I know what you're wondering," I said. "I hid in the
empty pantry till Roger came into the room then I jumped
out and well, you know…"

"The pantry?" asked Noah with a chuckle. "How could
you fit?"

"Well, the middle shelf was busted, so I had more
room."

"Don't you know her nickname?" asked Mom. "It's the
Shelf Elf."

Even Helen laughed this time.

"Can I see him?" asked Buster.

"Sure," said Celeste. "Come with me."

The rest of us lagged back in the kitchen to watch as
Buster walked into the family room.

"Mitch, this is Buster," said Celeste.

Mitch stopped bouncing in his armchair.

"Nnnngk."

The front legs of the chair left indentations in the rug
placed under and in front of the chair. Mitch wore black
sweatpants and a red, long-sleeved Husker T-shirt. Mitch
stared at Buster for a long moment. Then Buster tapped his
front pocket. Mitch stood.

"Clap, Mitch," said Celeste, who clapped.

Mitch looked at her then at Buster. He softly touched
his palms together. Buster reached into his pocket and
pulled out a cinnamon hard candy then held it out for
Mitch.

Mitch stepped forward, picked up the candy from Buster's hand and stepped back. He unwrapped it, letting the
wrapper fall to the carpet. He put the candy in his mouth
then smiled.

"Oooh-oooo!"

The tough felon's eyes moistened.

Mitch looked at the rest of us for the first time then retreated to the protection of his chair. Meanwhile, the rest of us gathered around Mom's pan of brownies. I introduced her to Noah and Ryan. She'd seen Celeste, Helen, and Kenny at the firm. The pounding started again as Mitch bounced back in his chair, lifting the legs off the ground. The family didn't seem to notice it. Celeste told Pearl that meant he was fine again.

"I've been reading a book by Temple Grandin," said Helen. "Of course, she's smart, but some things still apply. She says bouncing hard like that helps Mitch feel connected to his surroundings."

In time, Mitch wandered into the kitchen aware of something others thought delicious. Ryan took an old T-shirt out of a drawer and pulled it over Mitch's head. Then Mitch pushed past me to get to his chair. Kenny gave him a glass of milk. It was immediately clear why Mitch needed a special shirt for eating. He took a bite, ate it, but let the next one fall out of his mouth to the table. He then scooped that up and put it in his mouth as his long, thin fingers crumbled the rest of the brownie, much of it over the sides of the plate. Eventually, he picked up all the crumbs and ate the brownie, but not before he scattered then retrieved the crumbs. When he finished, Helen washed his hands and his lower face, and took off his eating shirt. Mitch started to leave the room when he stopped and looked at me.

"Yeah, buddy, that's the horse lady," said Noah.

Kenny handed Mitch a big, coffee-table book of horses. Mitch returned to his chair then whipped through the pages, eventually setting the open book on the floor in front of him. Across the double page was a black stallion.

I just smiled; the lump in my throat prevented any speech. Mom put her hand on my shoulder.

After we drove Pearl and Buster home, Mom was quiet. Finally, she cleared her throat.

"You wanted me to meet someone," she said. "It was Mitch, wasn't it?"

"Yeah. Judge Shelton rejected my petition for Kenny and Helen to become guardians and conservators of Mitch."

"But Kenny's been cleared of the murder charges."

"But Helen's in hot water. I'm only a step ahead of the State Patrol and FBI in learning that Helen is the ex-wife of Roger Harper. No one thought to investigate her."

"Was she in on it?"

"I don't think so, but it keeps things in limbo. I was hoping you would agree to be Mitch's conservator. Judge Shelton, your admirer, might agree to you as conservator with Kenny and Helen as guardians of Mitch."

"Helen and Kenny won't like my interference," she said.

"Not at first, but they may realize they don't have a choice. I'll stress to them that you have experience with a special needs young man and if you are the conservator, then the state won't try to make Mitch a ward of the state."

"They'd put him in a group home and he doesn't need that. Helen and Kenny seem suitable to me. Mitch looked happy there."

"And like Buster, Kenny will be getting his life insurance money. I'll make the request first thing Monday morning. So just think about it, okay? It's a commitment you'll be making until you die or lose your marbles."

"I'm pretty sure I'll say yes."

Jay drove out to my office before lunch on Monday.

"I bet you're not surprised about our investigation of Helen," he said as he looked out my office window.

"I confronted her last week about it. I know you need to look into it. It would be a shame if you found anything concrete. Mitch would suffer the most."

"Mitch, yeah. You've thought this through."

"I've always been intent on protecting that boy. He doesn't even know my name. I'll just be the 'horse lady' as Noah calls me."

"She's in deep trouble if she's found to have aided him."

"I don't think you'll be able to hang anything on her. Evidence would be a problem and I killed him. She says she didn't know about the scheme—and you killed the other evidence. She claims she only saw Roger when he first came to the house to visit Mitch. I don't think she was in the loop—what would've been the purpose? I don't know if she helped to hide him—again the evidence is dead. He certainly didn't hide in the Percival house…I'm certain one of the kids would've told on him."

"Did they know the first Buster was a fake?"

"No, but they didn't like him. They were all pretty young when they last saw the real Buster. And I told them he was a threat to Mitch."

"I agree. If Helen told Roger he might be able to hide in some abandoned farmhouse or barn, well, that would be hard to prove because she knows not to admit to it. Plus, I doubt there's a paper trail to find. Helen would've destroyed any evidence, thanks to your warning."

I smiled. "I don't care about Helen—like I said, it was all about taking care of Mitch. And she's good with him and Kenny's getting better."

"And I heard from Bill that you're sending Buster to truck driving school. No wonder Patty calls you the Fairy Godmother."

Chapter 26

A month passed. Despite four interviews, the FBI never filed charges against Helen. Meanwhile, Mitch adapted to his new home.

Winter transformed into spring—at least our strange Midwestern version of it. In April, Dexy's opened to moderate success that soon became the biggest attraction in the area on Friday and Saturday nights. Jay and I frequented Dexy's on Friday nights while remaining loyal to the Cowpoke on Saturday; even though we both preferred Tina's Top 40 selections to Johnny Two River's twang.

I blocked out the first two weeks in May for our trip to Europe with the understanding that I would contribute to the costs of the trip. I turned thirty in February and wanted to travel in comfort. As a college student, I didn't mind sleeping on the benches in European train stations, but I was dead set against travel hardship on this excursion.

On a weekend when it reached seventy degrees on Saturday and then snowed on Sunday, we lounged on my family room sofa. Jay turned to me in the fifth inning of a late afternoon Kansas City baseball game. The intense look on his face warned me of the topic.

"I still think we should get married," he began. "Let's look at the positives and the negatives."

As I sat up straight, my stomach cart wheeled. "Okay." I clutched a pillow to my chest and sat cross-legged.

"Regarding education and income—are we acceptable to each other?" he asked.

"Yes," I said.

"You are to me, but you don't even know what I make."

"I'm sure it's fine. But I have a confession. I possess a good chunk of money from my dad's life insurance—money I refused to share with Brian when we split."

"So what are we talking?"

"Well, I've spent some, gained some from investments. It's now more than the original death benefit of a half million."

"I'm impressed."

"I'd rather have my dad."

"I'd hope so. So, um, I'll give you a pre-nuptial agreement."

I hadn't thought of that, but that seemed fair. "Okay."

Then he cleared his throat to continue. "So, ah, sex—acceptable?"

"Yes, definitely."

"Yes, absolutely. I can make you glow in the dark."

I laughed.

"How about weirdness?" I asked. "On a scale of one to ten, I'm a seventeen."

"God gave you special senses. How many lives have you saved because of it?"

I shook my head. "My, ah, peculiarity, can torture me."

"I'm never going to completely understand it, but I want to help with the tough times. And I like the word 'quiddity' for it."

"What's that mean?"

"It means the inherent nature or essence of someone…your distinctive feature."

"Oh, yeah, I guess so. And how about employment?"

"You're a successful attorney, and I've seen you decrease your hours and your responsibility."

"It felt pretty crushing for quite some time. But it's better."

"How about me?"

"You have an impressive position with tons of responsibility. You work some long hours, but not always. I guess it depends on what's going on. But I'm not alone—I've got my gang, and can handle being alone…it's not the same as loneliness."

"Now how about downsides," he said.

"We haven't dated long," I said.

"And we've both had long-term relationships that we ended. That makes us cautious."

"You don't seem cautious to me. You seem ready to jump back into it."

"I've had more time to be ready to try again. I was plenty scared for a long time."

"My marriage fell apart just last summer," I said. "That's not long ago."

"Do you have any doubts that you did the right thing?"

"No, it needed to end. It was a relief. He wasn't up for the challenge of…me and I didn't want to try and carry him along. He became a burden."

"I'm ready for the challenge. I'm the man for you."

"We have been in a gunfight together."

"And had nightmares together," he said.

"I liked that you admitted you didn't want to be alone after the shootings."

"That was scary stuff. I was afraid for you and for me— the life and death double whammy. I wanted to hide in your arms, but I had to stay and be the tough cop for the others."

"While I went home and ate chocolate."

"I like those Belgian truffles, too. What else? Oh, children."

For the first time, I looked away from him. "I don't think I'm ready."

"But do you think sometime you'd want them?"

"I think I've progressed so that I can say yes, sometime and definitely more than one…one is lonely. I just don't know when."

"I can live with that. So how about family? Mine made a bad showing."

"But they're six hours away…so as long as they stay that far away, I'm okay with them. By the way, I made a peace offering of sorts. I sent Trish and Amy each a can of Pringles with a note that said not to eat the left side."

Jay let out a robust laugh. "Did you really lick them?"

"Nah. I just opened the seal to make them wonder."

"They'll think it's a hoot."

"So, how about my family?"

"Well, your family amounts to two…both winners."

"Two alive. I think Scott and Sweetie will always haunt me. And I'm always wondering, what would my dad do? Of course, the answer is nothing I've done. I keep getting in trouble."

"And getting out. Your dad committed a terrible blunder when he separated you from your mother and brother. That was enough for a lifetime. And you're not a bully. I heard he was. Though you're very protective."

I leaned forward and kissed him. "You're a good man."

"And I have something else I want to ask."

"Uh-oh. What's that?"

"I want you to teach me how to ride."

I laughed and agreed.

I kept this conversation in mind, particularly the morning after we arrived in New York. Our first stop was at Tiffany's, though he claimed we should stop there because we both liked the Audrey Hepburn movie. My guts started churning the moment we stepped out of the taxi, so the stop at a case full of wedding rings didn't surprise me, neither did the drops of sweat running down my back. He'd given me fair warning, so I was ready when the clerk covered the glass counter with a black velvet cloth and set a red box on it. Holly Golightly's remark about being too young for diamonds died on my tongue when Jay popped open the box. He took a truly stunning ring out of the box and turned to me.

"Megan Anne Docket, will you marry me?"

My body had gone to lead, so I couldn't bolt; no one came to offer me Belgian truffles; no Saint Bernard trotted to my side with a flask of brandy. So, I swallowed hard and delivered my well-thought out and exceedingly articulate answer:

"Yes."

Jay smiled, slid the ring on my finger then lifted me off the ground and kissed me.

I felt like we were the grand finale of some rom-com flick. Still, saying that one word made my guts stop roiling. My antiperspirant was done working for the day, but I could deal with that. While I was looking at men's wedding rings, he walked a few steps away and made a phone call. He wouldn't let me see how much he spent on my ring, so I sent him away while I purchased his ring.

Without a doubt, the man could plan. We took a taxi to a nearby Methodist church where a minister and an organist were waiting. We spoke our vows, the organist and the janitor witnessed the marriage license, and soon we were on our way back to Tiffany's to get the rings sized. His actually fit, but mine wasn't even close. Jay spent a ton to get the ring ready for me to pick up before we left for London.

I'd said that one earth-shaking word: "yes" and I knew it would change my life forever. We'd gotten that out of the way so we could enjoy our vacation, which now became our honeymoon. One word. Then I realized the three words I'd never said to him. So I pulled down his arm to stop him from hailing a taxi.

"Jason Andrew Young?"

"Yeah?"

"I love you."

About the Author

JUDY Bruce is a resident of Omaha, Nebraska, USA, where she lives with her husband, daughter, and autistic son. She has a law degree from Creighton University. Judy is the author of the Wind Series: *Voices in the Wind, Alone in the Wind, Cries in the Wind, Fire in the Wind* and future stories in the series, as well as *Death Steppe: A World War II Novel*. She maintains a website at judybruce.com and a blog at heyjoood.com.